"Don't worry over what your fiancé will say."

Greg's advice made Leonie bristle. "I'm not worrying about what Oliver will say!"

"Oliver!" Greg repeated scathingly. "God help us—what a name!"

"You know nothing about it!" Leonie raged. "What right do you have to make remarks like that?"

"As your temporary if slightly phony husband, I'd say I had a perfect right to comment on who's going to follow in my footsteps," he said, and laughed, making her fizz with temper.

"Oliver won't be following in your footsteps," she threw back, and Greg's smile vanished.

"Dead right, he won't," he said angrily. "I don't know why I'm involved with you at all. Hell, I must be crazy! I've got enough problems without adding a dizzy, blue-eyed blonde!"

CHARLOTTE LAMB
is also the author of these

Harlequin Presents

374—THE SILKEN TRAP
380—A FROZEN FIRE
387—THE CRUEL FLAME
393—OBSESSION
401—SAVAGE SURRENDER
404—NIGHT MUSIC
412—MAN'S WORLD
417—STRANGER IN THE NIGHT
422—COMPULSION
428—SEDUCTION
435—ABDUCTION
442—RETRIBUTION
448—ILLUSION
451—CRESCENDO
460—HEARTBREAKER
466—DANGEROUS
472—DESIRE
478—THE GIRL FROM NOWHERE

and these

Harlequin Romances

2083—FESTIVAL SUMMER
2103—FLORENTINE SPRING
2161—HAWK IN A BLUE SKY
2181—MASTER OF COMUS
2206—DESERT BARBARIAN

Many of these titles are available at your local bookseller.

For a free catalogue listing all available Harlequin Romances and Harlequin Presents, send your name and address to:

HARLEQUIN READER SERVICE
1440 South Priest Drive, Tempe, AZ 85281
Canadian address: Stratford, Ontario N5A 6W2

CHARLOTTE LAMB

midnight lover

Harlequin Books

TORONTO · LONDON · LOS ANGELES · AMSTERDAM
SYDNEY · HAMBURG · PARIS · STOCKHOLM · ATHENS · TOKYO

Harlequin Presents first edition September 1982
ISBN 0-373-10528-2

Original hardcover edition published in 1982
by Mills & Boon Limited

CHAPTER ONE

FROM the air the tropical forest looked like a dark green knotted mat, stretching on for mile after mile without a break. Although at first Leonie was fascinated by it she found the unending vista tended to pall after an hour or so, and began to wonder what would happen if the pilot of the little four-seater plane had to land in an emergency—which was a mistake, because once she had envisaged disaster in one form she went on to envisage it in others. Leonie had a very vivid imagination. As if she had conjured up the threat of it Joe, the pilot, suddenly looked over his shoulder at her, grinned and said: 'I'm going to have to put down. Sit tight.'

Leonie sat as tight as she could, her heart in her mouth, and was deeply relieved to see a small airstrip below them. They circled it several times before they descended, the wind of their passage making the treetops bend and dance. Leonie shut her eyes and held on to the arm rests, feeling perspiration breaking out on the back of her neck and trickling down her spine, making her thin cotton shirt stick to her. What am I doing here? she wailed inwardly and it did not help to know that she had nobody to blame but herself.

The plane wheels touched the earth, the plane bounced, skidding slightly, the whole structure shaking as it righted itself and taxied across bumpy, uneven ground.

'Okay, you can relax now,' said the pilot, laughing as he looked round at her and caught that screwed-up expression. He switched off the engine and turned to watch her as she released her seat-belt and stretched out, her legs shaking.

'You're the most unusual passenger I've ever carried,' he said, grinning from ear to ear. 'And, baby, I've flown everything from priests to crocodiles, but this is the first time I've ever flown a blue-eyed blonde out to the Mission.' He took off his headphones and ran a hand over his hair, smoothing it down. 'If it's not a rude question, how old are you?'

'Twenty,' Leonie said, and smiled at him as he shook his head in wry envy.

'I wish to God I was,' he said in a drawl.

'You're American, aren't you, Joe?' Leonie asked tentatively, having already learnt it was safer not to ask too many personal questions out here.

He nodded. 'You mean I still sound as if I hail from Idaho? I'm so used to talking French to everyone that I'd forgotten how to speak English.' He had a slow, dry way of talking which had amusement running through it all the time. Brown eyes, brown hair and a deep tropical tan made him a study in monochrome and made it difficult to guess his age, but she imagined he was in his late thirties.

'Are you ever homesick?' she asked, and when he grimaced, asked: 'Why don't you go back home, then?'

He looked out of the window at the blue sky, the black jungle crowding around the perimeter of the airstrip. 'I often ask myself that,' he said slowly, then his eyes lifted to the arc of the sky, the palms and liana vines twining around the mahogany trees which towered above thick dark bush. 'There's something about the place that gets you, I guess. I came here just after the French handed it over to the locals. I was flying for the government for a while, but it didn't work out—I have a rooted dislike of working for governments.' He grinned at her, his teeth very white against his brown skin. 'So I started out on my own and I've been scratching a living here ever since.'

'Do you get many passengers?' Leonie's face was doubtful and he winked at her.

'Not many, no. I fly freight inland, mostly. I do a regular run to the mines and I pick up heavy freight from the plantations.' He clambered out of his seat and opened the door, trod down on the wings and turned to help her climb down. Leonie was annoyed with herself because her legs were trembling and she found it hard to stand, she had to clutch at Joe's arm to support herself.

'Are you okay?' he asked, looking down into her flushed, perspiring face, and she nodded quickly. She didn't want him imagining that she was not fit for this trip. It had taken her long enough to persuade him to fly her out to St Xavier's in the first place. He had stared at her incredulously and asked why she wanted to go there, to such a remote area. Only when she had confided something of her reasons had he agreed, her offer to pay him a bonus on top of the fare he usually charged had not swayed him in the least. She had got the strong impression that Joe was his own man and not to be bought.

An ancient lorry was bouncing towards them over the baked earth. Joe glanced towards it and waved, getting a wave back from the dark-skinned man driving it. 'When we've refuelled we'll go on,' he told her. 'From here it's only an hour to St Xavier's, but I was fresh out of gas. Why don't you stretch your legs, honey? Don't go out of sight, though, the jungle's full of creepy-crawlies.' He leaned over and took the hat she was carrying, jammed it forcefully down on her soft blonde curls. 'And keep that thing on, you hear?'

Leonie laughed, her wide blue eyes limpid. 'I hear,' she said, and wandered away from the plane, staring at the blackness of the jungle which surrounded the tiny air-strip. From above you couldn't see it until you were right overhead, the tops of the trees seemed to dominate the landscape.

She couldn't believe she was actually here, so far away from her home in England. Ever since her plane from London touched down in Cairo she had been living in another dimension, her mind dazed by the constant assault of strange sights and sounds. She had spent a night between planes in Cairo and hadn't slept a wink, even after she had reluctantly gone up to bed in her hotel after a leisurely tour of the city with an English couple whom she had met on the plane and who had offered to show her the sights. They had been very worried to hear her plans and had tried to talk her out of them, but Leonie had more backbone than you might think. She had a hidden core of strength people didn't suspect as they looked at her slender, fine-boned body and the delicate oval of her small face between those blonde curls.

Her stepfather hadn't suspected it, although he had known her since she was five years old. She halted, staring at the bamboo thicket bending very slightly in a faint breeze, whispering as it moved. Her brows drew together in an anxious frown. It had taken a lot of courage for her to stand up to Thomas Lincoln, he was a domineering and autocratic man. Leonie had been saying yes to him all her life and she hadn't been sure she would find the nerve to say no for once. He hadn't been able to believe it, either. Both of them had been taken aback, but of the two of them, Leonie suspected Thomas Lincoln was the most surprised.

'The whole idea is crazy, simply crazy,' he had protested. 'You haven't set eyes on him since you were two, you don't even remember him. What do you expect to find? He walked out on you and your mother. If he cared anything about you, he would have tried to get in touch, but he didn't. You're going on a wild goose chase.'

'I have to see him, don't you understand?' She had stopped trying to put it into words by then, she had been forced to realise that her stepfather either didn't understand what she was saying or didn't want to try. She had fallen back on repeating those few phrases: 'I have to see him, I have to find out what he's like.'

Thomas Lincoln had been both hurt and bewildered as well as angry. He had been a kind and thoughtful father to her for most of her life. Leonie was deeply attached to him, although she was a little scared of him. She had learnt very early that so long as she did what Thomas Lincoln told her he would always be pleased with her. She had been showered with everything a girl could want—her own pony, pretty clothes, toys and a bicycle, and as she grew up even her own car. Her stepfather made no secret of the fact that he doted on her. He had no children of his own, so when he married her mother he had legally adopted Leonie and she used his surname without ever thinking about it. It wasn't until her mother died a year ago that she had discovered that her own father was not dead, as she had been told, but had been divorced by her mother and was living in a tiny independent state in what used to be French West Africa, on a remote Mission station.

'I'm your father,' Thomas Lincoln had insisted, staring at her angrily. 'He doesn't deserve to be called your father. He deserted you and your mother.'

Leonie had been close to tears. She had hugged him and tried hard to make him see why she had to go and find the man who was her real father, but too much had obscured their viewpoints from each other.

'What about Oliver?' her stepfather had demanded. 'Doesn't he matter, even if I don't?'

'You do matter, of course you do. I love you.'

'You've got a funny way of showing it,' he had growled, his heavy iron-grey head thrust aggressively towards her.

'Why won't you see that this is nothing to do with how I feel about you! But Pierre Denis exists, he's my flesh and blood father, and I've no idea what he looks like, what sort of man he is.'

'I'll tell you what sort of man he is—the sort who walks out on his wife and leaves her with a two-year-old kid,' Thomas Lincoln had said bitterly. 'Have you discussed this with Oliver? What does he say?'

'I'm going to tell him tonight,' she had said, and seen a spark of relief in Thomas Lincoln's eyes. He had hoped that Oliver would talk her out of it, of course, and Oliver had tried. For the next few weeks he and her stepfather had brought every conceivable sort of pressure to bear, but in the end Leonie's sheer determination had won out. She had begun to make the arrangements for her trip: book air tickets, hotels, have the necessary inoculations and get visas. She had written to her father at the Mission telling him she was coming, but had received no answer.

'He doesn't want to see you,' her stepfather had, predictably, told her. 'Can't you admit it, Leonie? The man is just indifferent, you don't mean a thing to him.'

From behind her, Joe shouted her name and she turned, sighing. Maybe they were quite right, maybe she was going on a wild goose chase to find a man who couldn't care less about her, but what they didn't understand, what she couldn't tell them, was that Leonie was going to find herself, not just her real father. Finding out that the past was not quite as simple as she had believed had altered something inside her. Her mother had lied to her all her life, so had her stepfather. Somewhere in the world existed a man to whom she was tied by blood closer than she was to anyone else alive, but she knew no more about him than his name. The shock of finding out that he was alive after all had been traumatic. It had made her re-assess everything in a new light—herself, her mother and stepfather, and even Oliver, because, to her amazement, she had found out that Oliver had known, he had been told years ago. The only one who hadn't known the truth was herself.

Why had they all lied to her? She could understand her mother suppressing the truth when Leonie was small, but why go on lying? She would never have found out the truth if she hadn't overheard the family solicitor talking to her stepfather—and even then, her stepfather's reaction had made it plain that he would have gone on lying if he could have convinced her.

'Hurry up, baby, we're ready to go,' Joe shouted, waving his arms towards her, and she started back towards him.

She was a few feet away when they both heard the sound of an engine wheezing towards them. Joe turned and stared, his hand masking his eyes from the blaze of the sun.

'Now, who the hell's that?'

A battered-looking jeep was coming at quite a pace, steam rising from the bonnet, with a black man in a small skullcap driving it and beside him a broad-shouldered white man leaning forward to stare at them.

As the jeep pulled up clouds of yellowish ochre dust swirled up around them and Leonie coughed, turning her head away, missing the moment when the white man leapt out and spoke in rapid French to his driver.

The jeep backed and as Leonie looked at him, the white

man dropped a case on the earth and offered his hand to Joe.

'Hi, how are you, Joe?'

'I don't believe it,' Joe muttered. 'Well, I'll be damned!' He grinned from ear to ear as he shook hands vigorously, clapping the other man on that wide shoulder. 'What in the name of Lucifer are you doing back in Mameea? Last I heard, you were in Cairo.'

The other man nodded. 'So I was—until my ears started twitching.'

Leonie listened, bewildered and curious, and saw Joe give him an odd intent look, his face changing, his eyes suddenly very serious and searching. 'Oh, yeah?' he asked, and the two men exchanged a long look which Leonie could not read.

The other man gave a casual shrug. 'Could be another false alarm, who knows?'

'No smoke without fire,' said Joe in a slow voice.

'Sometimes a fire can smoulder for years without bursting into flames,' the other said cryptically, and Joe inclined his head as though agreeing. He was frowning, but as his brown eyes slid sideways towards Leonie and she saw the worried expression in them Joe's face changed again, rather too rapidly, as though he was deliberately forcing a smile, as he noticed her wide-eyed puzzlement.

'You carry very interesting freight these days, Joe,' the other man drawled, and Joe laughed.

'Don't I just? Beats crocodiles, doesn't it?'

'But could have a bite that's just as deadly,' the smoky voice murmured, and Leonie found herself looking into mocking grey eyes whose dark pupils were rayed with tiny flecks of gold. The sun was shining into them and to her surprise she saw herself mirrored on the glassy surface of the iris, a tiny miniature of herself imprisoned in his eye for a second until he moved his head and shaded his eyes to look directly at her. The reflection of herself vanished from his gaze yet she felt she was still captive there, trapped behind his grey eyes.

'Are you talking about me?' she asked in a faintly breathless voice, angrily aware that she was blushing like a teenager under that amused gaze.

'Were we, Joe?' he drawled, and Joe laughed.

'Would we do a thing like that? Leonie, this is an old friend of mine, a buddy from way back. He comes and goes like the swallow, I never know when I'm going to see him flying back. Greg Thornton,' he ended, waving a hand between them. 'Leonie Lincoln.'

Leonie shyly put out her hand and after a brief pause it was swallowed into the strong brown fingers. She had to put her head back to look at him, he was a good head taller than herself, a tall, powerful man with the tautly muscular build of someone very active. His black hair was thick and windblown, his tanned face not exactly handsome but a face you knew you would remember, the features hard and yet full of a wry humour, faintly cynical, which fitted the assertive masculinity.

'Greg's a roving reporter for one of the London dailies,' Joe told her. 'A trouble-shooter—he covers most of the West Coast of Africa, but he's based in Cairo.'

'That's a long way from here,' said Leonie, smiling, and the grey eyes watched the gentle curve of her naturally pink mouth with interest. Leonie had given up wearing make-up on her journey, she found the heat made her perspire so much that her make-up was soon ruined, and as her skin gradually acquired a pale golden tan she looked just as good without it.

'By plane it's only a day away,' Greg Thornton said. 'Where do you spring from?'

'England,' she said, and he laughed softly.

'Well, who'd have guessed it?' he mocked, and her colour deepened. 'And what are you doing out here in the back of beyond?'

'Leonie's on her way to St Xavier's,' said Joe before she could answer, and Greg Thornton's dark head swung his way then moved back to survey her, narrow-eyed.

'St Xavier's? What on earth do you plan to do there?'

'It's a private matter,' Leonie said, her pleading gaze moving to Joe and begging him not to disclose the reason for her visit. She had had to confide in him, but she did not want anyone else knowing, and, for some reason, that especially included this large, cynical-eyed stranger whose height and self-assured manner made her feel both very young and very gauche.

Greg Thornton shot Joe a look, but he didn't press the matter, his shoulders moved in a wry shrug instead.

'Forget I asked. Mind if I share your plane? I'm going inland myself and it would save me a lot of time and trouble if I flew. When we've dropped you, Joe could take me on into the savannah.'

'Of course,' said Leonie, although her nerves prickled uneasily at the thought of sharing the rest of the flight with this man.

'I'll pay the rest of Joe's charge,' he said. 'The paper gives me a pretty free hand with expenses.'

'I've already paid him,' Leonie told him. 'Please don't worry about it, I'm glad to help.'

He studied her briefly, then nodded. 'Thanks, maybe I can do the same for you on my way back. How long are you staying around here?'

'I've no idea, I haven't decided yet.' Although his hard face showed not a flicker of expression as he listened she got the strong feeling that he was weighing up everything she had said, but what he was making of it she couldn't guess.

Joe moved restlessly, his feet sending up a little spurt of yellow dust. 'We ought to get moving, time's against us—I don't like flying in the dark and if you want me to take you on to Koum I'd like to get there before the sun goes down.'

'Okay,' Greg Thornton said, calmly turning to Leonie and seizing her by the waist with both hands. She gave a suppressed gasp and felt laughter in him, although she didn't see his face. He lifted her up on to the metallic wing and she clambered back into the plane and sat down, furious with herself for that involuntary little cry of shock. He joined her a moment later and stowed his case behind the seats, strapping it down. Leonie clicked home her seat-belt and out of the corner of her eye watched him as he took the seat next to her and fastened his own belt. Joe took his seat and a moment later the engine fired and the propeller revolved noisily. Leonie wanted to close her eyes, as she had the last time they took off, because she hated this moment. Once they were up in the air she was able to relax, but the moment when the tiny craft shuddered its way into the sky seemed perilous to her.

She kept her eyes down, staring sideways at Greg Thornton's lean brown hands as he opened a newspaper which, she could see, was printed in French and pre-sumably was a local paper. His long legs were stretched out in front of him and his body casually at ease as though he hadn't a care in the world. It didn't bother Greg Thornton to be flying in a lightweight aircraft apparently held together with sealing wax and string. She envied him that casual, lazy indifference to any possibility of disaster, but she was frankly cold with fear, the palms of her hands clammy as she pressed them together.

A hand reached out suddenly and closed over both her own. She looked up, startled, her huge blue eyes stretched to their limit, the thick gold-tipped lashes flickering rapidly as she tried to conceal the panic inside her.

Greg Thornton gave her a cool, reassuring smile. 'Joe has flown this plane more times than you've had hot dinners and, as you see, he's still in one piece.'

Leonie forced a smile, her lips quivering, and nodded. 'He's a marvellous pilot.'

'What would you know about it?' he mocked without unkindness. 'But you're right, he is—nerves of steel and no imagination.' His smile was charming, the grey eyes intimate and the words murmured in a low, confidential tone that wouldn't reach Joe's ears.

Leonie shook her head. 'I think he has got imagination—he talks so beautifully about this part of Africa, he obviously loves it. He's just brave, that's all. The more imagination you've got, the harder it is to be brave.'

'And you've got plenty of imagination,' he commented, staring at her, the warmth of his skin lying against hers as his hand rested on top of her fingers. 'You should have left that particular commodity at home in England. Africa is surprising enough without being seen by a kid with imagination.' He paused, then asked in a tone which was almost rough with abrupt impatience: 'How old are you, for heaven's sake?'

'Twenty,' said Leonie, and he gave a deliberate, mocking wince.

'Ouch, forget I asked. You shouldn't come around here flaunting that age in people's faces!'

She laughed, seeing that he was teasing her. 'How old are you, then?'

'That's a very personal question.'

'You asked me,' she defended, and he leaned closer, lowering his voice still more.

'You won't tell anyone?'

A little dimple appeared at the corner of her mouth. She shook her head while he watched her, intent on the smooth-skinned curve of her golden cheek, the surface lightly dusted with tiny blonde hairs which were almost invisible except at close quarters. Her skin had a freshness and colour which betrayed the fact that she came from other climes and the faint tan she had acquired had merely deepened the blue of her large eyes and the tender pink of her happily curved mouth. Leonie had hardly been touched by life yet, she was emotionally half asleep, and it showed in the almost childlike directness and yet shyness of her expression. When she smiled her mouth took on the curve of natural high spirits and the smile was reflected in her eyes.

'I'm thirty-eight,' he whispered, his mouth very close to her ear, sending a strange tremor of awareness through her at the warmth of his breath on her skin. 'But if you ever tell anyone I'll skin you alive!'

She had to look at him to make sure he was still teasing, and the grey eyes were alight with laughter.

She laughed back. 'I wouldn't dare, you're much bigger than I am.'

'You'd better remember that,' he said softly, then in a calm easy fashion asked: 'Now tell me something—why are you going to St Xavier's?'

Her body jerked in surprise at the sudden question and she drew back in her seat, bending her head away and conscious of the intent survey on the vulnerable curve of her neck.

'I told you, I don't want to talk about that.' She was angry because, fascinated by those grey eyes, she had almost found herself blurting out the truth and he had done that deliberately, he had lured her into liking and trusting him with that mocking smile only to spring his question without warning.

He leaned back, releasing her, but he went on watching her. 'There aren't many white people at the Mission. In fact, as far as I know there are only two—I wonder which you're going to visit? It can't be the priest, Father Armand, because he's French and as far as I know he has no English connections. So it has to be Dr Denis—but he's French, too, or so I thought. His English is very fluent, though, and he did live over there once, years ago.'

Leonie listened, fighting to keep her face empty of all reaction. She knew he was staring all the time, his eyes probing her profile to pick up some information.

'I've only met him twice, he isn't a very forthcoming character, he tends to keep himself to himself. I don't know much about him.'

'Perhaps he doesn't want you to know much about him,' Leonie retorted, prickling. 'Everyone has the right to their own lives, don't they?'

He shrugged, the movement sending a slow ripple over his wide shoulders and making her aware of the muscles under that dusty white shirt, which bore evidences of his long journey along bush roads, on rough badly made surfaces rutted and covered with the drifting yellow dust which, Joe had already told her, at the rainy season turned to a thick yellowy red mud and made the roads impassable.

She shifted further in her seat and looked out into the burning blue of the sky and far below them the clotted jungle, a dark green mat which gave no light to the forest floor beneath the thickly interleaving trees. There was no break in sight, but as the little plane flew on she saw a few clearings, the yellow thatch of roofs, whitewashed mud walls, and here and there a baobab tree whose wide branches gave shelter to native women as they prepared a meal out in the open.

'I hope you know what you're doing,' Greg Thornton said suddenly beside her. 'Who let you come all this way alone? Are your family out of their tiny minds?'

She looked round, her rounded chin lifted in defiance as his words reminded her of her stepfather and Oliver. 'I'm an adult, I've a right to make my own decisions!'

He stared, his lips twisting crookedly. 'They tried to stop you, did they?' he guessed, and she bit her inner lip.

'Oh, you think you're so clever!' she broke out in a resentful voice because he had come far too close to the truth.

'What sort of family do you have? Father, mother, brothers and sisters?'

She hesitated, but there was no reason why she shouldn't tell the truth about her family. 'My mother's dead, I've no brothers and sisters.'

'But you have a father,' he guessed shrewdly. 'And he didn't like you coming out here?'

Leonie looked away, and at that moment the engine began to make a thick, coughing noise and the light craft distinctly wobbled in the air, making Joe exclaim under his breath and Greg Thornton sit up, shooing a quick look towards the control panel.

'What's up, Joe?'

'Not sure,' Joe muttered. 'Thank the lord we're nearly there—I'll be able to check the engine on the ground, I've got a feeling the feed pipe is clogged with dust, it shouldn't take me long to fix.'

Leonie was very pale, listening to the noise of the engine, and Greg Thornton glanced at her. 'Relax, relax,

Joe will get us down okay. It's nothing serious, it happens all the time out here. All sorts of minor problems come up in the jungle—dust gets everywhere, and when it isn't dust, it's rain or mist.'

Over his shoulder Joe said: 'Don't look now, the sun's just setting. Afraid we'll have to make an overnight stop at the Mission. Greg. I'm not flying on wonky engines in the dark.'

'Okay,' Greg Thornton said casually. 'That suits me.'

It didn't suit Leonie, it worried her. She did not want Greg Thornton around with those cynical eyes and shrewd, quick brains when she met her father for the first time. It was going to be hard enough to face Pierre Denis and tell him who she was—she did not want any witnesses.

Joe was coasting down, the engine still coughing, and Leonie felt her mouth dry as she contemplated the possibility of crashing. Out of the window she saw the great orange ball of the sun rushing down the sky as if it was on fire, streaks of gold and scarlet colouring the deep purplish shadows behind it, and by the dying light she saw the thatched roofs of the Mission clustering around a tiny church with a white stone cross raised above the main door. On the ground people were moving excitedly, the gaudy colours of robes flaring like banners against the dust, then the plane flew on to the rough airstrip marked out between palm trees which whipped to and fro at the wind of their passage.

Leonie squeezed her eyes shut as the ground rushed towards her. When the plane's wheels touched the earth the plane tilted slightly, nose down, and ran on, bumping and bouncing, throwing her about as if she were a rag doll. Greg Thornton moved to clamp her against him, an arm around her shoulders, her face turned into his shirt.

Under it she heard the steady, rhythmic beating of his heart, telling her that he hadn't turned a hair, it hadn't entered his head to be afraid.

Her own heart was leaping about inside her like a live frog and she was trembling violently.

Above her head she heard Greg murmur: 'We're down, honey, you can stop shaking,' but she couldn't stop, her body would not obey the command of her mind.

She took a deep breath, furious with herself for behaving like this, and lifted her head away to give him a tight, painful little smile.

'I'm fine, thanks.'

He regarded her with indulgence, then took her chin in one long hand and raised it, brushed her mouth with his own lightly.

'Good girl!'

Leonie felt the hot colour flying up her face to her hairline. She drew away as though she had been stung, feeling the light pressure of his lips against her own intensely.

'What's the matter?' he enquired, his mouth indenting in mockery. 'Never been kissed before? There's a first time for everything.'

'Of course I have,' Leonie muttered. 'But I'm not in the habit of kissing strangers.'

'I shouldn't acquire it,' he advised drily. 'It could get you into trouble.'

Joe was leaning back, breathing noisily. 'Whew, I had a nasty feeling for a while there, but safe down is safe down, thank God.' He screwed his head round. 'You okay, Leonie?'

'She's okay,' Greg Thornton answered for her. 'She had an exciting experience, didn't you, Leonie?' His teasing eyes told her he was not referring to the near miss the plane had had with disaster, and Leonie looked back at him crossly.

'Not that I noticed,' she said, and he laughed. Joe looked rather bewildered.

'Did I miss something in this conversation?'

The cockpit door was flung open and a deeply tanned, weatherbeaten face lined with grooved wrinkles from care and anxiety, appeared in the doorway, smiling at Joe.

'Hello, Joe, we weren't expecting you to drop in on us—don't tell me you've got a surprise delivery for us? Father Armand's been praying for a miracle—I suppose it isn't a package of medical supplies from the port?'

'No, Doctor,' Greg Thornton said lazily, his glance moving between Leonie and the newcomer. 'This is our surprise delivery.'

Leonie felt all the colour rushing out of her face so fast she felt she was going to faint. The man in the doorway stared at her across the small plane, his face enquiring, puzzled, then suddenly the expression altered drastically. His eyes rounded, his lips parted on a thick gasp. Leonie could not move or speak, she could only stare, and the silence dragged between them like a dead body, heavy and inert.

CHAPTER TWO

It was the man in the doorway who finally broke the silence, his voice strained and uncertain. 'Leonie?' He whispered the word and then said it again a little louder. 'Leonie? Is that you?'

She managed to force a smile, her lips trembling crookedly, aware of Greg Thornton staring hard, his brows drawn together in a black frown. Why did he have to be there? She did not want anyone watching this moment.

'Yes,' she whispered back, and the doctor's face looked even more shocked, as though hearing her voice added to the whole impact of their meeting. The way he was looking at her made her realise that if anything he was more moved than she was; he almost looked as if he was afraid he was suffering from an hallucination.

'It can't be,' he muttered. 'It's impossible—you haven't changed.' His hand touched his own face while he kept staring at her. 'I don't understand.'

She was taken aback, puzzled. 'I wrote—didn't you get my letter?'

'Letter?' he repeated. 'No, I haven't had any letter.'

Joe shuffled his feet and the doctor looked round at him as though just remembering he was there. 'Why don't we talk in the Mission? Leonie's very tired, we've been flying for hours.' Joe said.

Still with that dazed air, the older man nodded. He turned and the aircraft rocked as he stepped out on to the wing and jumped down. Joe followed him and Leonie moved to do so too. A hand closed on her arm, detaining

23

her. She looked round, up into Greg Thornton's face.

'What the hell's going on?' he asked in a low voice, frowning. 'Look, are you sure you know what you've got yourself into? There's something about all this I don't like.'

'Nobody asked you to like it, Mr Thornton,' Leonie said unsteadily. All her attention was fixed on the man who had just left the plane, she had none to spare for anyone else at that moment. She was impatient of Greg Thornton's interest, his curiosity, she did not want him interposing himself between her and the man who was her father. She didn't yet know how she felt, herself; she certainly did not want a stranger examining her unknown feelings under a microscope.

She looked away, pulling her arm free, and walked down the plane, her head stooped a little because the roof was so low. Greg Thornton came behind her, his long body bent far more, and Leonie jumped down with Joe holding her hand, his fingers gently squeezing hers in silent reassurance. She smiled at him gratefully and he gave her a wink. She barely knew him, her explanation of why she had come all this way had been nervous and stammered, yet she trusted him and his relaxed manner was soothing. She felt he was an ally, someone she could rely on to help if not to understand, and she needed to feel that someone was on her side. Joe's support was untinged by criticism, he asked no questions, accepted without comment, whereas she instinctively knew that Greg Thornton would always feel free to comment. He might help her, but he wouldn't stop there, he would prod and pry and demand to know what she was up to and why, and then he would make his views very clear. She had spent most of her life under the domination of one strong-minded man, she was not about to allow another one to push his way into her life.

The airstrip ran close behind the Mission enclosure, and as Leonie turned towards it she saw a boy in a thin white robe lighting paraffin lamps, their crude glare showing her the mud walls of the buildings and leaving black areas outside the circle of light, thick shadowed places where lighter shadows moved, talking to each other in their own tongue.

Dr Denis was waiting, the night breeze ruffling his thin hair and the clean but faded khaki shirt he wore. Leonie walked towards him while he stared at her.

Joe fell behind, discreetly, and as Greg Thornton jumped down from the plane, took his arm to detain him.

As she joined him, Dr Denis said huskily: 'It took me a few minutes to work it out.' He gave a strange little smile, his mouth crooked. 'You see, when I first saw you, I thought you were your mother.'

She hadn't expected that. Her eyes widened. 'Oh, I see. But I don't look like her.'

'You're her image,' he said in a very quiet voice.

'I'd never thought so.' Leonie thought about her mother briefly, frowning. She had had silvery hair, a lined brow, a calm quiet way of speaking. Leonie could not imagine her at twenty. She had been forty-six when she died, and that was how Leonie remembered her; a neat, capable housewife whose world revolved around her home.

Dr Denis stared ahead at the compound towards which they were walking over rough ground. 'Did she send you? How is she?'

Leonie caught back a little gasp. She paused, searching for the right words, and he turned to look at her. As their eyes met all her attempts to say it gently were lost and she blurted it out.

'She's dead.'

He stopped in his tracks, stiffening. There was a long pause and the two men walking behind them caught up with them. Leonie felt Greg Thornton staring from her to her father, still trying to work out what was going on; why didn't he mind his own business? She was so absorbed in feeling her father's obvious shock that she glared at the other man, wishing he would walk on, wishing he wouldn't keep looking at her father as he fought with whatever emotions were keeping him silent.

'When?' Dr Denis asked in a thickened voice.

'A year ago, I thought they'd written, told you. I can't understand it.' She didn't understand anything, that was why she was here, because there were too many hidden things in her own life, things she did not know anything about, which had been deliberately kept from her. The past is always the parent of the present and the future can only spring from both. Leonie could not turn her back on that secret past, she could not think about her own future until she knew what her parents had never told her.

'No,' Dr Denis said, 'I didn't know. Nobody bothered to let me know,' and there was an unmistakable bitterness in his voice, the lingering tang of smoky regret, pain, a feeling she sensed but could only guess at.

'Are we going in or not?' Greg Thornton asked, those watchful eyes on her face.

'Of course, I'm sorry,' Dr Denis answered quickly, and moved on into the compound. Leonie looked quickly round at the buildings, saw dark faces watching her in turn, lustrous dark eyes gleaming in the lamplight, white teeth appearing in a broad smile as she met them.

'They're dying to know who you are,' Dr Denis told her, his face softening as he saw how she stared and was stared at. 'We don't get many visitors.' He suddenly smiled, his whole face changing. 'In fact, I don't think we've ever had a visitor like you before.'

'I'd say not,' Joe agreed, grinning. 'Pretty blondes don't drop out of the sky much around here.'

'Which is just as well,' Greg Thornton said drily, but Leonie ignored him.

'Where's Father Armand?' asked Joe, glancing around.

'In the sick quarters—malaria, he had to go into the swamps to visit a dying man last week and got a bad dose, worse than anything he's had before. He gets it every year, usually in the rainy season, a souvenir of the five years he spent in Gabon.' He turned and looked sharply at Leonie. 'You've had your shots, I hope?'

'Yes, before I came.'

'While you're here you must always remember to take your salt and quinine tablets.' He gave her a wry smile. 'I'll check on you to make sure.'

'I won't forget, I was warned about the dangers in the tropical forests.'

'Something tells me you weren't warned strongly enough,' Greg Thornton observed.

Dr Denis turned towards the nearest building, a square mudwalled house roofed with palm thatch, a narrow wooden verandah running the length of it, with a half dozen wooden steps leading up to it, the whole structure built up on wood piles to raise it off the ground.

'This is where I live—come in, all of you, I'll get my boy to fix you a meal and find beds.'

'Anywhere will do,' Joe said cheerfully. 'I must be up at first light to fix that engine. It was giving trouble as we came in, but I expect it's the usual. The other day I almost pratfalled when a damned great bird flew right into the radiator—feathers everywhere!'

Leonie shuddered and Joe laughed at her expression.

'Was it killed?' she asked, and all the men grinned at each other.

'I'm afraid so,' Joe said indulgently. 'So was I—almost. It nearly took the propeller right off.'

The wooden steps were rough-hewn and creaked as they trod up them, the thatched roof rustled overhead and as Leonie glanced up at it, Greg Thornton said laconically, 'Rats,' making her go pale.

'Really?' She wasn't sure he was telling the truth, her wide eyes searching his face.

Dr Denis opened the loosely swinging door and looked back at her, 'We do get a large number of vermin in the house,' he admitted. 'If you see anything, yell. They're more scared of you than you are of them.'

They had entered the low-ceilinged square room a few seconds later and Leonie stood staring around her in fascinated curiosity. A boy with very black skin and a loose white robe was lighting a lamp in the centre of a table. He straightened and gave them a little bow, smiling at Joe, who grinned back, and said something in what sounded like French, but a French Leonie did not understand. Seeing the way she was frowning, her father turned and said: 'Our people speak a mixture of their own tongue and French—you never know what words they're going to pick up. It just depends which ones take their fancy. But even if they don't speak French, they usually understand most of what you say. You may not realise it at times, they can look blank when they choose, but if you're ever in doubt, use French and you'll get by.'

'The French owned this territory for years, didn't they?' she asked.

'For almost a century, yes, and they left their mark all over it. Apart from the language, a lot of other influences were left working away here.'

'Yes,' Greg Thornton said drily, and Dr Denis gave him a frowning look, his brows raised.

'I wonder what brings you back here,' he said, and Greg shrugged.

'I followed my nose. If I'm wasting my time again, I can soon get back to Cairo, but there was nothing cooking around there and it's always good to keep your eye on a boiling pot.'

Dr Denis sighed. 'Let's hope the pot is nowhere near boiling.'

'I'll drink to that,' said Joe, and Dr Denis laughed, his face relaxing.

'Is that a hint? Well, I do keep the odd bottle, purely for medicinal purposes, of course.'

'Of course,' Joe agreed, grinning.

Turning to the boy, Dr Denis said something in that thickly glottal language and the boy inclined his head in a dignified way, moving to the door.

'Sit down, Joe, Mr Thornton,' invited Dr Denis, waving a hand at the rather uncomfortable-looking cane chairs which had shabby, faded patchwork cushions for up-holstery. 'Leonie, I'll give you a quick tour of the bungalow while we wait for the drinks.'

She followed him out of the room into a narrow corridor. He opened a door and showed her a tiny room containing a tin bath and a very primitive lavatory. 'The best we can do, I'm afraid,' he said, looking slightly uncomfortable. 'Would you care to . . .'

Leonie flushed, nodding. It had been a long flight and she had been wondering how to phrase the request.

'The kitchen is down the end of the corridor, I'll wait for you there,' Dr Denis told her, walking away.

She closed the door, pulling the piece of motheaten string hanging down the wall. A naked light bulb flickered overhead, came on dimly. By its light she saw something move in the tin bath and choked back a scream as she realised it was a huge hairy black spider. It kept trying to climb the straight metal sides and falling back. Leonie stood at the door, peering under the bath and into every corner before she felt safe enough to move.

When she joined Dr Denis he was tasting something in a large blackened pot on an antique-looking range. He looked round and offered her the metal ladle. 'What do you think?'

Gingerly she tasted it. 'Oh, curry,' she said. 'Rather nice, what sort of meat is it?'

He eyed her wryly. 'One doesn't ask. Just eat and be thankful, as Father Armand would say.'

The kitchen was dominated by a large table and a cracked ironstone sink with an incongruous red plastic bowl filling it. A basin of fruit stood on the table and beside it an open metal tub of uncooked rice grains.

'Mtali is quite a good cook,' Dr Denis told her. 'He came here because he had appendicitis, he would have died if he hadn't walked through the jungle to get here, and he decided he liked it here and wanted to stay. The only job he fancied was cooking, I'd hoped he would work in the hospital, he's very gentle and methodical, but he doesn't like Soeur Bernadette. Mtali won't take orders from a woman—he's very proud.'

Surprised, Leonie exclaimed: 'Then there are women here!'

'Of course,' her father said. 'I have three nurses, thank God. Very good ones.'

'Mr Thornton said there were no women at the Mission.'

Her father frowned. 'He was wrong, then.' He looked at her with dry irony. 'I imagine he meant white women—my nurses are all local women, I trained them myself. I had a French nurse, but she cracked under the climate and had to go home, so Father Armand went over to a convent on the coast and came back with four volunteers from the nuns. He managed to get them because this is a Mission station as well as a hospital. They're serving God out here. One of them hated it, too. She went back to the convent, but we manage without her.'

Leonie looked down, biting her lower lip, wanting to ask more questions but not even sure what she wanted to know. 'Why are you here?' she asked at last. There was so much about him she did not know, but how do you walk into a man's life after eighteen years and say: tell me about yourself, I need to know.

There was a silence while he gazed at her, then she looked up and saw that calm irony in his face. 'Why are you?' he asked, and she smiled tremulously, shrugging.

'I'm not sure—because you are, I suppose.'

He nodded, rubbing a thumb along his sallowed skin. 'I think I see. You're full of questions, I imagine. I don't even know if I can give you any answers, but maybe you can give me some.'

'That's very cryptic,' Leonie murmured, laughing.

'You're young enough to imagine life has answers,' her father said in a gentle voice. 'I'm old enough to wonder if I ever knew the questions.' He studied her and she met his eyes directly, the blue iris clear and very deep. 'You look so like your mother,' he said huskily, 'I can't believe it. Every time I look at you I see her. I'm too off balance to talk tonight, my dear. It's been a shock to me. Can we postpone the question-and-answer session?'

She nodded, moistening her dry lips with the tip of her tongue, rather relieved not to have to pursue the matter.

Maybe she would know what it was she needed to find out if she waited a while.

'You're nervous?' he asked, watching her, and she nodded again, forcing a smile. 'Don't be,' he said, putting a hand on her slender shoulder, his thin fingers firm and reassuring. 'I'm glad you came, Leonie, I've often wondered how you had grown, what you looked like.' He stopped short, grimacing. 'I had no right to wonder, did I?' His eyes watched her and Leonie met them again, that question in her stare. He sighed. 'Later—we'll talk later, when I can put it into the right words.'

'It isn't easy, is it?' she said, half to herself. 'Words never seem to come out the way they should, they're supposed to link us together, make us understand each other, but they don't, they often keep us apart.'

'You think too much,' he said, and his face was pleased; the words might sound like criticism, but his eyes showed that he liked that. He moved to the door, then halted and said with his back to her: 'Your mother—what did she die of?'

'She had a heart attack,' Leonie told him. 'It was all over in two minutes, they told us. She just died.' Leonie had been at work when it happened, her stepfather had rung her to break the news. She had gone home in a dazed state of shock and disbelief. 'She was in the garden playing with our dog,' she added, as though that made it more real.

'She was never strong,' Dr Denis mused. 'She had rheumatic fever as a child, her heart always gave trouble.'

'I didn't know that,' said Leonie, surprised, 'She never told me.'

'She refused to admit it, even to herself,' he said. 'They warned her never to have a child, but she had you.' He stopped short again.

'I suppose that's why she never had any others,' Leonie mused, thinking back and remembering other things which she hadn't even known she had noticed. Her mother had often been pale after some exertion, her step-father had always been very protective, insisting that his wife must rest after a long walk, must not play tennis in the summer heat. Leonie had put all that down to his autocratic nature, but now she wondered.

'Didn't she?' His voice sounded rough, again she heard that emotion very near the surface, but she couldn't be sure what it was. He opened the door. 'Come and see the bedrooms.'

There were two very tiny bedrooms, each with an iron-framed bed in it, draped with mosquito netting, the floor stained dark brown, a few native mats strewn on it. The windows were shuttered, but the air was full of that droning sound which Leonie already knew meant there were mosquitoes at hand, dive-bombing you when you least expected it. One buzzed around her head and she flapped a hand to drive it away.

'Tiresome little pests, aren't they? I've got some repel-lent cream somewhere, I'll find it for you. They don't trouble me much any more. I'm afraid you're likely to be very plagued by them.' He led her back into the sitting-room where they found Joe and Greg Thornton drinking whisky, talking quietly. Both men looked up and smiled at them, but Greg's eyes were sharp, far too penetrating for Leonie, who looked away from them.

Greg leaned over and pulled a book out of the row of rather mildewed volumes beside his chair. 'All your books are French, Doctor.'

He smiled. 'French is my original language—I'm a half-caste.' There was mischief in his face. 'My father was French, my mother English, I've lived in both countries.'

'But you think in French, obviously.'

'I rarely have time to think at all here, I'm too busy. This is the only hospital for a hundred miles.' Moving to the bottle of whisky, he poured himself a small glass. 'What about you, Leonie? I'm afraid I've nothing else.'

She shook her head and Joe laughed. 'Very wise,' he said. 'And remember, if you drink the water make sure it's been boiled.'

The door opened and the tall, dark boy came in with a glass of pale yellow liquid which he offered to Leonie with a shy smile. She took it, smiling back. 'What is it, Mtali?'

He looked at the doctor, who asked the question in the native tongue and got a smiling reply. 'He says it's squeezed citrus juice,' Dr Denis explained. 'Lime and lemon, probably. The fruit we grow here is very limited— bananas, of course, and dates, and citrus of one kind or another.'

'Thank you, Mtali,' smiled Leonie, sipping. 'It's delicious, very refreshing.'

Her father translated and Mtali smiled and went out, adding something as he went.

'Dinner will be in a quarter of an hour, when he's boiled the rice,' Dr Denis said.

'Mtali's cooking is always worth eating,' Joe told her. 'Even when he serves curried lizard.'

'Lizard?' Leonie repeated, aghast.

'Don't tease her,' Dr Denis smiled. 'Take no notice of him, of course it isn't lizard, although lizard is delicious, I assure you—it's an acquired taste, though, and you won't have to face it tonight. I expect we're having some sort of bird—chicken, possibly, I noticed some wing portions in the pot. Native birds often look like chickens and Mtali is an expert trapper. He goes off into the jungle at first light to catch our dinner.'

'Do you really eat lizards?' she asked, not sure whether to believe him or not.

'Certainly, the bigger ones are rather like chicken to taste—no, actually they taste rather like wild rabbit.'

She shuddered. 'Don't tell me if there's any lizard in the curry tonight, I think I'd rather not know.'

'Nice to be able to close your eyes to what you don't want to see,' Greg Thornton murmured, and she looked at him, flushing.

'It can be a very wise self-protective mechanism,' her father said in a clear, stern voice, and Greg looked up and met his eyes.

'I'll sort out somewhere for you to sleep tonight,' the doctor told him, walking to the door. 'Mtali has put your case into your room, Leonie, unless you would rather spend the night in the nurses' quarters? The three nuns have a house of their own next door.'

'I'll be happy wherever you've put me,' she said quickly. 'I don't want to cause too much trouble.'

'No trouble, I'm giving you Father Armand's room. I've put him in the isolation wing of the hospital, he needs constant nursing and I can't spare one of the nuns to watch him over here. He won't mind you using his room for a few days.'

Greg listened, watched, his eyes constantly moving from one to the other. Her father went out and Joe got up and sauntered over to pour himself another small whisky. Mtali came into the room and said something to him thickly. Joe made an irritated face and glanced at the other two.

'I've got to go and set a guard on the plane—Mtali says some of the local kids have been hanging round it, and I don't want any of them meddling with the controls. They're far too curious. I'll be back in two shakes of a lamb's tail—wait dinner for me.'

'Need any help?' Greg asked as he moved to the door and Joe shook his head.

'I'll pay one of the men to watch the plane, it won't take five minutes to suss out which of them is the most honest.' He grinned. 'Lucky I've got some cigarettes with me.'

When he had gone, Leonie queried: 'Cigarettes?'

'A form of local currency,' Greg Thornton explained. 'They don't always trust money, but cigarettes are always acceptable.' He gestured with his glass. 'Whisky even more so.'

Leonie frowned. 'Oh, I see.'

He mocked her, his face hard. 'You see, do you? What do you see, I wonder?'

She didn't answer, sinking into the chair Joe had vacated, and linking her fingers in her lap, her head bent, aware of his brooding gaze on the windblown blonde curls.

'The doctor said you were only staying for a few days,' he probed.

'Did he?'

'A few moments ago, he said Father Armand wouldn't mind you using his room for a few says.'

'Yes,' Leonie agreed unrevealingly, twisting her pale slim fingers into a cats' cradle and unlinking them again, her brow furrowed with absorption in the small game.

'This is no place for a girl like you, especially now,' Greg Thornton told her forcefully. 'Take some advice— get back to the coast as soon as you can and fly back to England where you're safe.'

She looked up. 'What do you mean? Especially now?'

He hesitated. 'This isn't safe, secure little England— this is a very unstable country, anything can happen any time. Don't you know anything about this place?'

'Not much,' she admitted. 'What sort of trouble are you talking about?'

He sighed, his face uncertain. 'I'm not giving you a political history lesson. The government has a very shaky grip on the country, that's all, and there are rebel tribes on the other side of the inland savannah country who are always threatening to start an uprising.'

'That's why you're here,' Leonie guessed, but then she had guessed as much while he and Joe were talking in the plane. Joe had called him a trouble-shooter.

'That's why I'm here,' he agreed, finishing his whisky.

'Do you think these tribes are going to start anything now?' Her skin was prickling with cold perspiration and her voice wasn't quite steady. She had not bargained for getting caught in the middle of some sort of civil war when she came here.

He shrugged. 'I heard whispers—but then there are always rumours of that sort of thing, especially when a government is very unpopular.' He got up, nursing his glass, and she threw a look towards his face, his black head almost touching the low ceiling in the little room. 'Just make sure you're on your way out as soon as possible,' he said in a clipped tone.

Leonie swallowed, a peculiar tremor running down her back. 'Why do you live out here?' she asked. 'Your job must be dangerous.' Why did her father live here? His job must be dangerous, too, he must walk every day with death at his side—why did he stay, why had he chosen to come here?

'It isn't dangerous so much as potentially dangerous,' Greg Thornton explained, his eyes suddenly gleaming with an excitement she saw and found disturbing.

'And you like that?'

'I guess I must do or I wouldn't be here.' He put his glass down and moved to stand in front of her, his hands thrust into his trouser pockets, staring down at her. 'There's a magnetic pull about danger, although you wouldn't have discovered that yet. To be able to face danger you have to have common sense, be able to calculate the risks involved.' There was a reckless glitter in his grey eyes and she felt their stare with a quiver of alarm at something in them. 'For instance, take yourself.'

'Me?' she asked, bewilderment in her voice, staring at the hard tanned face and trying to guess what he was talking about.

'If I were a man inclined to take risks, I'd risk finding out if that cool little English face of yours hid anything more passionate than a love of walks in the country and tea by the fire.'

Leonie's colour rushed up her face, her eyes dropped away from his watching stare. 'But you're not a man inclined to take risks,' she said, managing to sound amused.

'Not without knowing what I'm getting into,' he agreed. 'I might be intrigued by the mixture of big innocent blue eyes and a cool, go-to-hell mouth, but I think I'd decide not to get my fingers burned with trying to handle such an explosive mixture.'

'Well, that's a relief,' she said, her chin lifting.

'Unless I had encouragement,' he murmured, very softly, watching her.

'Not from me, Mr Thornton,' Leonie assured him, looking up again. 'My fiancé might object if I had to confess I'd been flirting with another man.'

His brows drew together. He looked at her linked hands, the bare fingers. 'You don't wear a ring.'

'It isn't official yet, but when I get back to England it

will be.' It would have been official by now if she had not
decided to come to West Africa to find her father. Oliver
had been too annoyed with her to buy her a ring for her
twentieth birthday, as they had planned for months. Her
stepfather had insisted that she must wait until she was
twenty before becoming engaged and that they couldn't
be married until she was twenty-one, and Oliver had been
happy to wait. He too had felt she wasn't yet old enough
to get married, and anyway, Oliver always agreed with
Thomas Lincoln, they thought alike on every subject.
Oliver and Leonie had known each other all their lives—
Oliver's father was a partner in Thomas Lincoln's firm
and the two families had spent a great deal of time together. Leonie had never dated anyone else. It had always
been Oliver for her from the time she could run after him
and demand to be allowed to go wherever he was going.
He was five years older and the took the same protective,
indulgent, slightly autocratic attitude to her as her stepfather did.

'And he let you come all this way alone?' Greg
Thornton demanded in brusque, contemptuous tones.

'I'm not his property,' she retorted indignantly. 'I have
a will of my own.'

'He can't be much of a guy,' he said tersely.

She stiffened. 'You know nothing about it, about either
of us. Keep your opinions to yourself.'

'I never do,' he said in a suddenly amused voice. 'That's
what I'm paid for—handing out my opinions to the
world.'

'Well, don't bother on my account,' Leonie said crossly.
'My own opinions are all that matter to me.'

'Not those of your unofficial and absent fiancé?' he
drawled.

She refused to answer, but looked away, and he

watched her ruthlessly, trying to read her averted profile.

'So he didn't give a damn what sort of hot water you might be chucking yourself into?' he asked.

'Of course he cared!' she burst out. 'He was very . . .' She halted on the verge of admitting that Oliver had tried to talk her into giving up the whole idea, and Greg Thornton nodded his head.

'Uh-huh, he tried to stop you and you dug your little toes in, did you?' He leaned down towards her and murmured softly: 'Do you want to know what I'd have done in his place?'

'No, I don't want to know!' she muttered, the back of her neck prickling as he leant so close, the hard clarity of his face very near. His features had an austere cast, his tanned skin taut over his strong bones, the firm male line of his mouth drawing her eyes against her will, making her remember how it had felt when that mouth lightly touched her own and left an indelible mark she felt again now, a heat and pleasure she found very disturbing. He was unlike anyone she had ever met. Having him so close made a coil of helpless awareness tighten inside her body.

'I'm going to tell you, all the same,' he mocked, smiling, watching her all the time, the slide of his eyes down her face and body like the brush of fingertips, arousing pulses she had never known she possessed, beating at her neck, her wrists, her temples and deep inside her body. His voice lowered still further, whispered, taunted. 'I'd have shackled you to my wrist and kissed you hard every time you tried to stir an inch.'

Leonie's breathing was hard and fast and she had to struggle to control herself. She wanted to leap out of the chair and run, but she knew he would laugh out loud if she did, because her feminine instincts told her that Greg Thornton was deliberately mocking her, teasing and

needling her to amuse himself. He didn't mean any of
this and if she reacted like a prim schoolgirl she would
only amuse him still more.

'Luckily my fiancé isn't anything like you,' she said
coldly, and he laughed.

'I'm sure he isn't.'

'He trusts and respects me,' she added, lying in her
teeth and doing it without a blush. Oliver did not respect
her, he treated her as though she was a little girl, but she
wasn't telling Greg Thornton that.

'The man's obviously an idiot,' he said, and as he spoke
the door began to open. He moved calmly and without
haste towards the table and picked up the whisky bottle,
pouring himself a tiny amount into the empty glass, as
Joe came into the room, wiping his neck with a handker-
chief.

'All settled?' Greg Thornton asked, and Joe nodded,
apparently oblivious of the atmosphere in the room.

'I dashed one of them five cigarettes and he's promised
to keep the boys away from the plane.'

Dr Denis came back, smiling. 'Dinner's coming now,'
he said. 'I hope you're all hungry, Mtali has gone to a lot
of trouble for you.'

CHAPTER THREE

THE dinner was very good, the curry a little strong for Leonie's taste, bringing her out in a fresh wave of perspiration, but she was hungry enough for that to be no real problem, and if there was anything strange among the contents of the curry she wasn't looking for it. She told herself firmly that it was chicken she was eating and nothing else. The rice was very fluffy and beautifully cooked, and a bowl of home-made chutney stood beside a plate of sliced bananas, the flavour of the fruit cooling the heat in her mouth. Dr Denis laughed at her when she poured herself a third glass of the lime-flavoured drink which Mtali had served with the meal.

'Too hot?'

'Just a little,' she admitted, laughing back. 'But I like it.'

Joe took another ladle of curry, a beatific expression on his face. 'I don't often get cooking this good, my woman slaps any old thing in front of me.'

'Are you married, Joe?' Leonie asked, and blushed as all the men looked at her with dry smiles.

'Not so's you'd notice,' said Joe, unabashed. 'I'm not ready for leg irons yet. They chain you to one spot, and I like to feel I can make a run for it any time I like.'

'Is that how you feel, Doctor?' asked Greg, his eyes narrowed in that shrewd, probing stare which Leonie was beginning to recognise. He never let anything go, he worried away at it until he had an answer, and it annoyed her because he was examining something he had no right to know about.

'I've been tethered to one spot for fifteen years,' Dr Denis said calmly. 'Don't ask me.'

'But you never married,' Greg said. 'Did you?' There was a pause, then he said: 'Maybe you regret not having married.' Dr Denis still made no attempt to answer, his head bent while he ate his last mouthfuls of curry. Greg shot Leonie a look and she gave him back an indignant, bristling stare. Greg's grey eyes measured her thoughtfully, then moved back to the doctor as though deciding he was an easier target.

'You're still an active man, how old are you? Fifty? Not too old to marry and have kids. I've known older men than you marry and settle down after years of being a bachelor.' His voice was casual, but there was nothing casual about those eyes, he was watching intently to see what sort of reaction he was getting.

Dr Dennis pushed away his plate and leaned back, a wry smile on his suntanned face. 'No wonder you're one of the top foreign correspondents, Greg! Do you know what you remind me of? An anteater, always digging into things.'

'What am I digging into now?' Greg asked, quick as a whip, and Dr Denis laughed.

'Give it up, Greg. You're using the wrong tactics.'

Mtali came into the room and bent over to murmur into the doctor's ear. Sighing, Dr Denis nodded. He got up and said regretfully: 'Sorry, I have to go over to the hospital. Leonie, your room is ready whenever you want to go to bed. Make sure you seal yourself off behind the mosquito net, we don't want you eaten alive.' He looked at the men, gave them a smile. 'Mtali will show you the hut I've set aside for you. Sleep well. I'll see you before you leave tomorrow.'

Joe got up as the door closed behind him and yawned. 'Well, I'm going to hit the sack—I've got to get up at cockcrow and start fixing that engine. Coming, Greg?'

'Yes, sure,' said Greg, without moving. 'Give Mtali a shout to show us over.'

Joe nodded and went out. Leonie rose and Greg got up too, halting her with one hand on her arm.

'Promise me you'll be out of here within a week,' he said quickly.

'Why should I promise you anything?' she demanded.

His fingers tightened and she gave a faint gasp. 'Listen to me, you obstinate little . . .' He broke off, his mouth twisting. 'I'm wasting my breath, aren't I? Why are you here, anyway? What's going on between you and the doctor? Why all the secrecy? If you're some sort of relative, why hide it? What are you being so uptight about?'

'It never occurs to you that none of that is any of your business, of course!'

'It's my business when I see a blind little fool walking straight into a possible storm,' he bit back. 'You shouldn't be here, you don't belong in a place like this, you've no idea what you're doing.'

'I do,' she said angrily. 'I came because I had to, and nothing you say makes any difference. If any trouble starts I'll leave.' She drew a painful breath and looked up at him. 'Will that satisfy you?'

His face altered, he gazed into the huge dark blue eyes with an unreadable expression. There was a silence between them which she felt inside herself, a moment of intense awareness, unlike anything she had ever felt before. It was not merely a physical sensation; every nerve in her body was conscious of him as a male, the wide shoulders and lean tense body vibrating with masculinity as he stared at her, but it was a strange emotional recognition as though their eyes were talking, although what they were saying Leonie was not sure.

Greg put one hand to her cheek, brushed it lightly, the warm flesh only just touching her own so that the tiny golden hairs on her skin tingled under his palm.

'Joe and I may have left by the time you wake up,' he told her. 'We're unlikely to meet again. I'll probably stay up country for a while, it may take time for me to work out what's brewing.'

Her lashes flickered and she swallowed on a hard knot in her throat. She had only known him for a few hours, what difference did it make to her if she never saw him again? He was a man from another world, a world she had never even glimpsed until now. Every line in his face, in that tough tempered-steel body, betrayed the gulf between them. Leonie had been sheltered all her life, wrapped in the cocoon of money and protection which Thomas Lincoln had woven around her. Greg lived dangerously and enjoyed it, his cynical, hardboiled view of the world totally different from her own.

'I hate leaving without getting any answers from you,' he said on a wry note and she smiled at him, sudden teasing in her face.

'Sorry.'

His answering smile was mocking. 'There's one thing you can tell me,' he murmured softly, and she tensed.

'What's that?'

'This,' he said, and bent his head before she could take evasive action. When he kissed her in the plane it had been a light kiss for a child, but this time his lips took hers with a fierce demand which shook her to her depths. Instinctively she clutched at his shirt as she felt her body weaken in dazed reaction and his arm went round her and held her close to him, their bodies touching, her head forced back by the power of his kiss. It was over in a minute and he was moving away, leaving her stunned and shaking, but her senses were flashing her after-images of the warm, compelling movement of his mouth, the pressure of his thigh against hers, the feel of his fingers pressing into her back, and she was unable to speak or move.

He looked at her, his face faintly flushed, his eyes almost angry. His mouth tightened into a hard line.

'You don't even know what it's all about, do you?' he asked. 'Go back to England and marry your unofficial fiancé, Leonie. You aren't ready for real life yet!'

He was gone before she had time to take that in, the door closing with a controlled violence which she jumped at, her nerves beating with angry fire. Greg had kissed her and awoken feelings she had not known she could have, and then he had contemptuously walked away. Very flushed, she stood listening to his voice as he and Joe talked to Mtali in the corridor. The voices moved away and faded and the tropical night filled her ears with sounds: the drone of mosquitoes, the rustle of palms, the sullen whine of the wind through the trees beyond the Mission enclosure. Slowly she went out and made her way to her own little room. Mtali had left her case in the centre of the floor. She unpacked, hanging her clothes in the wardrobe which smelt of camphor and wood stained with insect-repellent varnish. The mosquitoes were already beginning to drive her crazy, her legs were covered with bites that itched abominably and she couldn't stop herself from scratching them. She washed in the enamel bowl on the old chest of drawers near the bed and got into her cotton nightdress. Sliding into the bed, she arranged the mosquito netting, hearing the mosquitoes' high-pitched whine outside it.

It wasn't easy to get to sleep. Her mind was over-charged with memories of the day, and beyond the shuttered windows she heard the night sounds which in the dark could seem so menacing, the constant whirring of insects, the sudden sharp cry of some wild animal in the encircling jungle.

Her face burned as she remembered Greg Thornton's mouth enveloping her own. She turned on to her stomach and pressed her face into the pillow, quivering from head to foot. Oliver had never made her feel like that—but did she want to have such feelings? When Oliver kissed her she felt happy, contented, loved—Greg Thornton had made her ache with a painful sensation she couldn't identify, and the burning ache still smouldered inside her, hurting and bewildering her.

Despite herself, she slept heavily all night, and woke in a room flooded with primrose colour from the rising sun. Leonie lay behind her netting, watching the sunrays piercing the closed shutters. The air was cool and alive for a few hours. These were the best moments of the day before the sun rose high in the tropical blue sky.

Pushing back the netting, she got up and washed, dressed in a shirt and jeans with boots into which she pushed the hems of the jeans to make sure no insect crawled inside. The humid air made her blonde hair hang limply in fine strands; her usual natural curl deserted her in this temperature.

She found Greg in the sitting-room, seated at the table, eating a sliced banana mixed with some sort of moist cereal which she didn't recognise. He looked up and gave her a head to toe survey under which she flushed and tingled with exasperation.

'Sleep well?' he enquired in a voice which merely added to her feeling of nervous awareness.

'Yes, thank you,' she said, sitting down opposite him and looking at the large bowl of cereal in the centre of the table.

'Try some,' he advised. 'It's rather like muesli and very good with banana. Mtali boils the milk. It's quite safe—it's goats' milk, of course, but it's quite good.'

'I think I'll just have a banana,' Leonie decided, taking one and peeling it. She poured herself some coffee and added the thin bluish milk. Sipping it, she decided it tasted all right. 'How's Joe getting on with his repairs?' she asked without looking up. Having Greg opposite made her intensely selfconscious.

'He started work at first light, but it's taking longer than he'd expected. He's a first-class mechanic—he has to be, he often only has himself to rely on.' Greg glanced at his watch. 'I must go out and see how he's getting on—he shouldn't take much longer. He'd just diagnosed the trouble last time I saw him.'

'Has he had breakfast?'

'He lives on coffee and fruit,' Greg said drily. He watched her sip her coffee, his eyes half-sheathed by lowered lids, and although she didn't even glance his way she could feel his gaze intently. She was afraid of meeting his eyes. He couldn't possibly guess that she had lain awake for hours last night thinking about him, reliving that kiss, but she was afraid he might glimpse how she felt in her eyes if he met them. She had only known him for one day, yet she felt oddly that he had altered something inside her, something she didn't yet understand.

The door opened and Dr Denis came into the room, his face cheerful. He smiled at them both and Leonie welcomed him with an eagerness born of relief that he was breaking up the uneasy intimacy of the moment.

'Good morning, isn't it a beautiful day?' she asked, and both men laughed.

'It almost always is,' said Dr Denis. 'Morning, Greg—Joe asked me to warn you he was leaving in ten minutes.'

'He's fixed the engine, has he?'

'It seems so. He was just going to clean himself up—he was covered with machine oil from head to toe.'

Greg grinned. 'Isn't he always? He loves fiddling about with his plane.' He got up, stretching, and Leonie involuntarily looked at him, helplessly aware of the powerful masculinity of his lean body. She could not imagine him in the drab setting of an English background. He had too much life, too much vitality.

'We'll come and wave you off,' her father told him, offering her his hand, and she got up obediently to walk out into the blazing sunshine.

Joe gave her a broad grin as they reached the plane and found him standing beside it, his hands on his hips. 'Hi there, so you weren't a mirage!'

'Did you think I was?' she asked, laughing.

'It crossed my mind. I have these little fantasies from time to time. This is the first time one of them came true. When I write home to tell them what I want for Christmas I'll ask for a blue-eyed blonde. My mother can get anything out of her catalogue, she says.'

Leonie laughed again. 'Well, good luck.'

'Are we on our way or not?' Greg asked curtly, and Joe threw him a curious look, nodding.

'Jump in—I'm just ready to take off.'

Greg shook hands with Dr Denis and gave Leonie a brief nod. 'Take my advice, don't hang around here too long,' he said as he turned and climbed into the little plane. Joe winked at her, patted her cheek lightly and followed him. Dr Denis drew her back towards the compound and they both watched the plane taxi away and a moment later rise into the blue sky. Leonie felt herself sighing, although why she should she did not know. She barely knew Greg Thornton—why should she care if he stayed or went?

She walked slowly back to the bungalow beside her father, feeling the unseen eyes watching them both from the other little houses. 'Joe promised to pick me up whenever I sent for him,' Leonie murmured as they climbed the rickety steps. 'You contact him by radio, don't you?'

Her father nodded. 'I told him I'd get on the air as soon as you were ready to leave.' They went into the shadowy passage, leaving the hot morning outside, and Dr Denis called Mtali. 'Make me some fresh coffee, will you, Mtali?' he asked, and Mtali nodded, smiling. As Leonie followed her father into the sitting-room, Dr Denis said to her: 'I'm happy to have you here, Leonie, but for your own sake it wouldn't be wise to stay long. Greg's right—there's trouble brewing, and I don't want to have to worry about you getting caught up in it.'

She nodded. 'I understand.' She glanced towards the window, her eyes moving over the blue sky through which Greg was winging at this moment. Would she ever see him again?

Her father sat down, sighing. 'I was up very late last night, I'm bone tired.' His thinning brown hair blew faintly in the morning breeze as he shifted, settling himself comfortably in his chair. 'Now, tell me why you're here, Leonie. It's a long way to come just to satisfy your curiosity about me.'

She sat down, too, very nervous now that the moment had come. She didn't know how to explain why she was here. After a little silence, she stammered: 'They lied to me, you see.'

He frowned, taken aback. 'Lied to you? About what?'

'They told me you were dead,' Leonie explained, and saw his face take on a drained, shocked tension.

'Dead?' he repeated in a low voice.

'I can't even remember when they told me—I always knew you were dead from as far back as I can remember. If I mentioned you, they said you'd died when I was two, of some tropical disease.'

Pierre Denis got up and walked to the window, standing there with his thin back towards her, staring out over the compound. Over his shoulder she saw the palm-thatch of the next house, the whitewashed mud walls gleaming in sunlight. A dull-skinned green lizard ran up the wall and poised there, pulsating in the warmth, flat against the surface.

'That was unforgivable of her,' he said huskily at last. 'How could she do a thing like that?' He sighed deeply, his shoulders moving. He had the wiry, tense strength of someone who is always at full stretch, hardly aware of his own body, all his energy given over to what he has to do. His hair was a dull, lifeless brown and showed patches of pale skin through the lank strands, his skin tanned by sun and wind to the texture of dry parchment.

'I believed them because I never saw you, you never wrote or came to see me.' Leonie fought to keep accusation out of her voice. She might have felt anger against him once, but not since she had met him, talked to him, looked into his quiet, caring eyes. Whatever he had done to her and her mother, Pierre Denis was a man she instinctively respected and admired. She didn't understand why he had walked out all those years ago, but she wanted to understand, and the fact that her mother and stepfather had lied to her for so long made her feel that there was more to the past than they wanted her to know.

'I can only tell you in my own way, will you listen and

try to understand?' He didn't turn round, his voice was very quiet.

'Yes, that's why I'm here—to find out the truth.'

'The truth?' he repeated, and laughed gently. 'In the jungle there are trees so tall you can't see the tops of them when you're standing underneath. They have roots as thick as a man's arm which snake away in all directions. Even if you chop the tree down you're never able to track down every root, they're too tangled.'

Leonie said nothing and he looked at her over his shoulder. She smiled at him. 'I do understand,' she said. 'Tell me what you want to tell me, your way.'

He nodded and leaned on the window frame, staring out. 'I met your mother when she was about your age—I was working in a London hospital on a year's scholarship studying tropical medicine. I was already planning to come out here. It was my great ambition, I was fascinated by Africa from an early age. When I realised I was in love with your mother I had to realise something else— she was petrified by the idea of living in Africa, she hated hot countries, and her great dream was to live in a nice house in a pleasant part of England.'

Leonie smiled to herself. 'Yes, that sounds like her.' Her mother had always been reluctant to do anything new, anything different.

'I had to decide which I wanted most—my dream of Africa or your mother.' He paused, sighing again. 'I chose your mother. We were married and I got a partnership in a practice in Surrey. Within a year I was bored stiff. I hated everything about the way we lived—except your mother, I still loved her, nothing could alter the way I felt about her, even when she met another man and fell in love with him.'

'Oh!' Leonie gasped, shaken, unable to stop the little cry.

Her father turned and looked at her wryly. 'She met Thomas Lincoln soon after you were born. It took me around six months to realise she no longer loved me, was in love with another man. He was all the things she really wanted—he was rich, ambitious, social-minded, he could give Leonie a beautiful home and status. They were the practical reasons why she wanted him—but don't think she just wanted what he could give her, I believe she honestly loved him, far more than she ever loved me.'

Leonie thought back over the years she could remember and nodded. 'Yes, I think she did, I'm sure she did, they were always happy.'

Pierre Denis gave a bitter smile. 'I'm glad about that.' Their eyes met and he grimaced. 'Oh, I am, believe me— I wouldn't want her to be unhappy. That's why I left. I saw we were in an impossible situation—neither of us happy as we were. Leonie was very conservative, she would never have divorced me unless I gave her a perfect excuse—she would have been scared of social scandal. So I went and she divorced me and married Lincoln. It was a tacit part of it that in giving up Leonie, I gave you up too.' He looked regretfully at her. 'As you see, this was no place for a child and you belonged with your mother. For years I shut out the memory of everything in England. I'm sorry if I ever hurt you, Leonie. I was selfish, too busy trying to heal myself to think of any wounds I might be inflicting on you.'

'There were none,' Leonie said, her brow furrowed. 'Because I thought you were dead.'

He looked at her sharply. 'Yes, of course. Then maybe Leonie was right, after all, to tell you I was dead.'

'No! It was a lie, and when I found out, it shattered me. They all lied to me, long after I was out of childhood.

They went on treating me as though I was a child, they had no right to tell me lies about something that import-ant.' She hadn't put it into words before, but now she did, knowing that that was what she had thought ever since she discovered the truth. 'They had no right to do it,' she went on. 'Once I grew up, they should have told me and let me decide for myself what I thought about it. Whatever their motives, they had no right to do it.'

'Is that why you flew all this way? To punish them for treating you like a child?' Dr Denis asked with a faint smile, and she felt herself flushing.

'I suppose so, in a way,' she admitted reluctantly. 'When I found out, it altered how I saw them all—my mother, my stepfather, Oliver.'

'Oliver?'

'We were going to be married, I've known him all my life, but he knew the truth and he hadn't told me, he'd lied to me without thinking. When people hide things how do you know what else they're hiding? How can you trust them ever again?'

Her father came back to the table and sat down, staring at her. 'That's a question only you can answer. I'd say it would depend on their real motives for lying in the first place. You have to assess what anybody tells you in the light of what's in their minds when they say it.'

'I'm not a child any more!' she said angrily.

'Maybe you hadn't convinced them of that, and maybe you're not sure of it yourself,' he suggested, and she thought about that, her brows knitted in a disturbed frown. 'We're not always sure what we are or what we feel, mostly we act on instinct, and luckily our instincts seem to carry us through,' he added, smiling.

Leonie fingered her coffee cup, pushing it gently and abstractedly, while he watched.

'Did you come here to find me or to find yourself?' he asked, and she looked up, laughing involuntarily.

'You're very clever, aren't you, Father?'

They were both aware that she had used the name for the first time and that she had done it deliberately. She had not called him that until now because she had still been unsure of him, wary of making another mistake.

'I wish I were,' he said drily. 'I'm just a man, Leonie, and your mother was just a woman—don't blame her for what happened, our marriage was a mistake from the start. I should never have married her, it was one of those ironic jokes of fate. I always loved her more than she loved me, but then it's rare for a couple to love equally. There's more often one who cares deeply and the other who merely accepts all that love without being able to return it. I don't think your mother was capable of deep feelings. She didn't even love Lincoln with any depth, I suspect, she just preferred him to me. Or am I fooling myself?'

'No, I don't think so,' said Leonie, seeing her mother as if from a great distance and seeing her more clearly, as a person instead of a cardboard figure labelled Mother. She had never seriously thought about what made her mother tick, she had seen her as a flat, one-dimensional personage who would never alter, had always been the same. She hadn't imagined her mother as a young girl with choices to make, feelings to cope with—now she had to accept that her mother had had faults like everybody else, she had been human and fallible; a woman, not merely a mother.

'I think,' she said slowly, 'she would probably have felt that loving someone to excess was rather vulgar.'

Dr Denis broke into surprised laughter, giving her a look which had a new appraisal in it. 'You're right, of

course she would. I don't think she wanted to hurt me—
she just felt trapped, and what had trapped her was the
way I felt about her. I asked too much, I wanted more of
her than she was prepared to give.'

'What a pity, she missed so much,' said Leonie involuntarily, then flushed. 'Sorry, I shouldn't have said
that.'

He surveyed her with a gentle smile. 'We aren't talking
like father and daughter, you know—but then we never
had a chance to do that, did we? And that's my fault. I
regret that.'

'But you don't regret coming here?' she asked, and he
shook his head.

'Africa gave me back all the love I never got from your
mother. I don't regret a day I've spent here.' He paused.
'I don't regret loving your mother, either—in the end,
loving is the only real thing in life, even when you get
hurt. I may have left her, but I never really said goodbye.'
His face was sombre and Leonie watched him, very
moved.

'Love is not love which alters when it alteration finds,'
she murmured, and he smiled at her.

'Shakespeare, isn't it? He's the only English writer I
have—all my other books are French, most of them
authors I read when I was very young. I'm too busy to
keep up with new ideas—the old ones have to do for me.
I don't have the equipment or the money for newfangled
medicine. My main instruments are my brains, my hands
and the luck of the devil.'

Leonie looked down, thinking that it was not only her
mother who had missed so much by sending him out of
her life. Leonie had missed a great deal, too. Fond of
Thomas Lincoln though she was, she had always felt a
distance between them, an inability to communicate

which she had imagined came from a generation gap but which, she suspected now, came from another cause entirely. From the first instant that she had seen her real father she had felt she knew him, they had begun to talk as though they had known each other for a long, long time. Their minds worked in a similar way, even when they weren't speaking, as now, she felt some sort of flow between them, a silent exchange of understanding which needed no words.

'I'm the only doctor for a hundred miles,' he said. 'Mostly the people rely on their witch-doctors, and very good some of them are—I've learnt a great deal from them about local herbs. Medicine started with chaps like them. Most of my patients are handed on to me by a witch-doctor who knows the disease is beyond them. They resented me at first, but once they saw I respected them, they respected me. I wouldn't say they love me much, but we keep a civil truce.'

'Will you show me your hospital?' she asked.

'Of course, why don't we go over now? Soeur Bernadette will be having her coffee and in a good temper.' He gave her a mischievous look. 'I'll tell you a secret, but never repeat it. I don't run the hospital, she does. I'm far more scared of her than I am of the local witch-doctors. She's a very formidable lady.'

Leonie laughed and collected her hat to walk with him across the compound to the thatched hospital building. A number of patients sat on the verandah, fanning themselves with huge green leaves to keep away the insects buzzing around their heads. They all stared at Leonie with unwinking curiosity as they chorused: '*B'jour, m'sieur le docteur.*' Despite their thickened accent the words were unmistakable and Leonie was pleased with herself for having managed to understand them for the first time.

He stopped and spoke to one or two, teasing them, getting broad smiles or rueful shakes of the head, then he and Leonie went into the building and he opened a door into a tiny office.

A very small woman in a spotless white uniform stood up from behind a desk. A cup of coffee stood in front of her, half drunk.

'*Bonjour*, Soeur Bernadette,' Dr Denis said very politely, and she bent her head, her smooth-skinned black face haughty.

'*Bonjour, je ne pensais pas te trouver debout à cette heure-ci.*'

'Can we speak English? My daughter's French is not good,' he said, watching the nun's face and obviously enjoying her look of sheer disbelief.

'Your daughter?' The black eyes inspected Leonie in surprise. 'I didn't know you had a daughter, Doctor.'

'I almost forgot, myself,' he said, and the nun's calm face betrayed a flicker of curiosity. 'Leonie is visiting us for a few days. She wants to see what we're doing here.'

'Would you like me to show her round the hospital?'

Dr Denis sat down and reached for the coffee pot, pouring himself a cup of coffee. 'Fine—I'll stay here and do some of the paperwork you're always nagging me to do.' He winked at Leonie. 'We have to order every single thing we use here, and pay in advance for it.'

'And then pray that we'll get what we've ordered,' the nun added as she opened the door. Leonie smiled at her as she followed her out of the office. Soeur Bernadette pushed open another door and Leonie followed her into a narrow, crowded ward.

'This is the surgical ward,' the nun said, pausing to look around. 'The doctor does more than is humanly possible with the equipment we have, but a great many of our patients refuse to believe he can heal them.

Superstition is still rife here.'

There were men and women in the ward; lying on straw mattresses without any form of bedlinen. Leonie followed the nun around the beds, glancing shyly at the patients, who either glanced shyly back or looked away, ignoring her. When they left that ward, they visited another, which was even more crowded, and Leonie met the other two nuns who worked there. The younger one barely spoke to her, but Soeur Angélique, the older of the two, smiled and nodded. She was a thin woman with a rough skin pitted by smallpox. She spoke very little English, but her face was gentle and she and Leonie managed to make each other understand with sign language and gestures.

Soeur Bernadette led her out and pointed to a third door. 'That is what we call our isolation ward—we keep it in reserve for patients who have contagious diseases. At the moment, Father Armand is in there. I expect your father would prefer to introduce you to him, so we will go back to my office, I suggest.'

Dr Denis was there, scribbling away, his empty coffee cup at his elbow and he looked up, groaning. 'At last—I was wondering how much longer I was going to have to sweat away at these forms. Joe brought some rolls of gauze, didn't he?'

'Yes, and some drugs—I've checked them into the supply room and locked it.' Soeur Bernadette grimaced at Leonie. 'We have to lock everything away or it is stolen— even here, drugs are highly prized, and, in the wrong hands, often lethal.'

'Far too often,' Dr Denis added, sighing. 'Leonie, come and meet Father Armand now—I told him you were here and he is eager to meet you.'

'I'm eager to meet him,' said Leonie. 'I've heard so much about him.'

'He founded the Mission, we joined forces ten years ago after I'd been working all over Mameea without having a permanent base. One man can't do much—and even with the wonderful staff we have here, our work is just a drop in the ocean.'

'Every drop counts,' Soeur Bernadette put in.

Dr Denis grinned at Leonie. 'Whenever I start to wonder if it's all worth it, she stiffens my backbone, even if she has to use a lancet on me!'

'May I have my office back now, Doctor, or are you going to waste some more of my valuable time in idle chit-chat?' Soeur Bernadette enquired tartly, and he roared with laughter.

'Idle chit-chat? Where did you pick that up? Been reading those women's magazines again, have you?'

She looked pink and confused. 'Certainly not!' she denied, and the doctor winked at Leonie.

'Come and meet Father Armand,' he invited.

She smiled at Soeur Bernadette. 'I hope I'll see you again later.' She got back another smile and added: 'Thank you for showing me the hospital.'

The nun nodded. 'Your daughter has better manners than you have,' she told Dr Denis.

Outside in the corridor, he whispered to Leonie: 'Somehow a pile of women's magazines got here from England, and she loves them. When you get back to England it would be a real kindness if you'd send her some. They're the only vice she has.'

Leonie laughed. 'Of course I will, I'll send a crateful.'

'No, no,' he said quickly. 'That would make the port authorities suspicious—no, a small parcel of them would be perfect. Any more would make her guilty, anyway. She has so little to be guilty about, I like to think she isn't quite perfect.'

Opening the door of the isolation ward, he looked in and said: 'A visitor for you, Father,' his face amused, and Leonie walked shyly into the small room and looked at the man sitting upright in bed with old, well-washed blankets heaped incongruously over him.

Father Armand was old, that was the first thing she noticed about him; a man whose age she couldn't even guess at, his brown skin withered and sere, his black eyes sunk deep in his head, his body thin to the point of emaciation. The second thing she noticed was his smile, which wiped out all thought of age, all thought of everything but the warm, steadfast humanity in those dark eyes.

'So you are Pierre's daughter,' he said. 'I'm very happy to meet you at last.'

Leonie smiled and then looked quickly at her father, her face asking a question. She had imagined that nobody knew of her existence, but it sounded as if Father Armand had known.

'Father Armand is my confessor, remember,' her father said, laughing. He walked over and took the priest's bony wrist between his fingers. 'How are you feeling?'

'Much better, it is passing off.' There was perspiration dewing the old man's head, his skin had a yellowy tinge to it, the whites of his eyes discoloured and bloodshot. 'Leave Leonie with me for a while,' he told Dr Denis, pulling his wrist away. 'It will be good to talk to someone who doesn't keep trying to feed medicine into me or take my pulse.'

'You ungrateful old man,' Dr Denis said cheerfully, walking towards the door. 'Leonie, make sure he doesn't talk too much.'

Father Armand pointed to a rickety cane chair by the bed. 'Come and sit down and talk to me, my dear.' He watched the doctor leave, the door swinging behind him, sending a brief wave of air across the tiny, suffocatingly hot room. The sun had risen overhead to its highest point now and the shutters had been closed, leaving the room shadowy.

Turning to her, the priest said: 'Now, tell me all about yourself, Leonie.'

She looked doubtfully at him, wondering what to say, and he smiled. 'Well, tell me about your family first—what sort of man is your stepfather?'

Surprised, she stammered: 'He's very generous.' It was the nicest thing she could think of to say about Thomas Lincoln. He was open-handed, so long as she pleased him, but he was a man who liked his own way and liked to manage things—his firm, his own life and that of everyone around him. It was his great gift, the ability to manage affairs, it was what had made him so successful in the business world, a sense of organisation, a grasp of how things worked, how people worked, and he used it ruthlessly. The fact that he did it with a certain charm, a cheerful manner, made him difficult to defeat. You could only do it by being obstinate, immovable, and that made him angry. Angry, Thomas Lincoln was no longer quite so charming.

But Leonie didn't intend to say all that to the priest, she meant to skate over the subject as lightly as possible. It was only when she left him that she realised just how much she had somehow told him. He wheedled it out of her so gently, so imperceptibly, that at the time it escaped her notice that she was more or less telling him the whole story of her life.

Mtali came to tell her that the midday meal was ready, and she said goodbye to the priest and followed the light-moving young man across the compound to the doctor's bungalow.

The meal had to be eaten alone—Dr Denis had been called away, she was told, to attend someone in a nearby village. When Leonie had eaten the spicy strips of pork boiled in a thin sauce, the mound of white rice, she felt oddly sleepy and went to her room to rest in the sweltering afternoon heat. With the shutters closed and the mosquito netting in position, she curled up on the bed and fell asleep within minutes, her dreams a confused riot of impressions of all that had happened to her in the last few days. Through the dreams the figure of Greg Thornton moved briefly, and again she felt that painful mixture of excitement and alarm, her body twisting anxiously on the bed. She woke up perspiring, trembling, and lay listening to the whirr of insects outside in the merciless sunshine. Greg Thornton might have gone out of her life for good, but he had left a thorn under her skin and it hurt.

CHAPTER FOUR

OVER the next few days Leonie found herself settling into the pattern of daily life at the Mission. She woke up each morning in time to eat breakfast with her father, put on a hat and went for a walk with him around the compound before they went into the hospital. Soeur Bernadette allowed her to help with some small jobs in the wards—washing patients, taking temperatures, making beds, and even helping to feed those unable to feed themselves. Leonie soon discovered that in the little hospital there was always a job waiting to be done—there weren't enough hours in the day for all the work which piled up.

The nuns moved softly, without haste, having learnt that to hurry in the tropics is to perspire freely, and Leonie imitated them because she soon realised that their calm way of moving killed two birds with one stone. It soothed the patients who lay, almost hypnotised, watching the stately unhurried form of Soeur Bernadette as she progressed around the ward.

When she was not working in the hospital, Leonie helped Mtali in the kitchen, at his own shy request, his eyes cast down as he stammered in French that he wished to learn new ways of cooking the scrawny local chickens and the tough, highly flavoured pork which needed strong spices to make it palatable to a European taste.

'Mtali's so shy,' she said later to her father. 'He barely looks at me.'

'That isn't because he's shy,' Dr Denis said drily. 'Mtali despises women, he must want to learn to cook very much if he's prepared to ask for your help.'

'Now you've disillusioned me,' Leonie said, laughing. 'I thought he was very sweet.'

'Mtali's as bright as a button,' her father told her. 'I wish I could coax him into the hospital to work with me, I could do with an assistant, but he just won't take orders from a woman, so that's out.'

'But he asked me to help him!' she pointed out, and her father gave her a smile.

'You're my daughter,' he said, and left it at that, but it was Soeur Bernadette who gave Leonie some glimpse of how highly her father was regarded in Mameea.

'His name is known from one end of the country to the other,' the nun said as they worked together one day, bandaging a wound which made Leonie feel sick. The man who had come in to have his machete cut stitched looked impassively at the wall, pretending the two women were invisible, but there was sweat on his forehead, she noticed. 'Your father is a great man,' Soeur Bernadette told her, straightening. 'He has little help and few drugs, but he saves hundreds of lives every year.'

Leonie started and brushed an ant off her leg, looking down gloomily at the big red welt its bite had left. She was getting used to the constant attacks of insects. Soeur Bernadette looked down, too, and said: 'Ants again—get the bucket.' Several times a day they had to wash the ward down with disinfectant, and each piece of furniture stood with its legs in little tin cups of paraffin to discourage the ants from climbing on to the beds and chairs. Life in the hospital was an unending battle with the forces of nature—and nature too often won.

After dinner each evening, Leonie's favourite time of the day arrived, when her father and she sat down to talk in the dim light of the naked bulb hanging from the ceil-

ing. The shutters were closed against the warm, tropical
night, the whine and buzz of insects didn't seem to matter,
Leonie was too fascinated by what her father said. He
made her laugh with anecdotes about his adventures in
the jungle, kept her tense with suspense as he remembered
moments when he had come close to disaster, gave her
some idea of the ties which bound him to this place when
he talked about Mtali and Soeur Bernadette and Father
Armand. She realised more and more how strongly they
all felt about each other—they were a tightly knit little
family, working, nagging, quarrelling, teasing each other.

'I wish I could stay here,' she said one evening, and Dr
Denis regarded her with his customary wry amusement.

'I wouldn't allow it,' he told her bluntly. 'This is no
place for someone like you, the climate would kill you
inside a few years. Don't even consider it. No, you must
go back home, where you belong. I'll miss you, you've
brightened us all up, but you'll write, won't you? It won't
be goodbye, just au revoir,' He grinned at her. 'And
there's Oliver waiting for you at home, remember.'

Leonie smiled back. 'Yes, there's Oliver, but he seems
so far away.' Her father's eyes were even more amused by
that.

She was not confessing to him that since her arrival at
the Mission she had spent more time thinking about Greg
Thornton than about Oliver. The admission, even to herself, made her colour rise. She was unlikely ever to see the
man again—why couldn't she get him out of her mind?
She had known Oliver almost all her life, she barely knew
Greg Thornton at all. The way he kept haunting her was
ridiculous.

Next morning, Mtali woke here with a light tap on her
door and she sat up, yawning, in the pale dawn light,
calling: 'I'm awake, Mtali!'

They were going to the nearest market that morning. It was, Soeur Bernadette had told her, a weekly event to which everyone for miles around looked forward.

Leonie got up, washed and dressed and then joined Mtali in the sitting-room. She had discovered that he spoke a few words of English which he had picked up from the doctor and they were able to have strange conversations in a mixture of French, English and sign language. This morning he gestured to a flat brown loaf which lay in the centre of the table and said: 'Bread, mees. We go soon.'

'Thank you, Mtali,' said Leonie, sitting down and pouring herself some coffee. She cut herself a slice of the bread, which had a nutty, crunchy texture unlike anything she had ever eaten before. Mtali had put some goat's cheese and mango jam on the table, and Leonie ate a little of the soft white cheese. She had just finished when Soeur Bernadette arrived, smiling. 'Good morning,' she said, and refused a cup of coffee. 'We must hurry,' she pointed out as they went out of the bungalow into the compound, which was filling with a faintly misty radiance of light. The flash of orange darting across one side to the other startled her and she followed it, eyes dreaming.

'A swallow,' Soeur Bernadette informed her, and Leonie looked at her incredulously.

'A swallow? That beautiful little bird?' Used to the drab brown and grey of London sparrows, she couldn't believe her ears but the nun laughed and insisted that it was a local swallow.

'They are many colours here,' the nun explained, and looked up into the sky which was veiled with an opalescent haze, pink and blue and gold, the delicate drifting mists fading away as the sun began to rise. 'This is my favourite hour of the day, before the heat begins.' She looked round

as they both heard a spluttering, coughing sound, and to
Leonie's amazement a very old jeep crawled into sight
with Mtali seated at the wheel. The vehicle was battered
and sagged visibly on its wheels, the protesting note of the
engine like the wheeze of a very old man who isn't quite
sure he can move another step, but it was moving, and
when it stopped beside them, the nun gestured for Leonie
to climb into it. Dubiously Leonie perched in a corner,
her knees almost under her chin, while Soeur Bernadette
squeezed in beside her. The jeep jerked and shuddered
and began to move with the utmost reluctance.

They turned out of the compound on to an earth road
which wound between towering mahogany trees from
which flew a multitude of birds whose colours staggered
Leonie and kept her silent, staring up at the branches and
their noisy, excited inhabitants, hardly daring to look
away in case she missed something. Birds were not the
only occupants of the trees—she saw monkeys swinging
like chattering acrobats eager to have their skills admired,
flying squirrels swooping like Dracula from one patch of
black shadow to another and small lizards which lay
against the rough tree trunks so unmoving that she
thought at first they were discolorations on the bark until
sunlight hit them and showed her a round, unwinking
eye. As the day began the sounds from the interior of the
jungle intensified, but she could see nothing beyond the
first ranks of trees, the entangling liana and the heavy
suffocating blackness of the deep forest making it impossible to make out any living thing.

Climbing up hills was a task almost beyond the old
jeep, which croaked and whined and begged for mercy as
its tyres spun slowly in the choking red dust, but when
they finally did reach the top of a hill it would give a
whimper of relief and Mtali would let it coast down at an

ever-increasing speed, the almost defunct undercarriage
bouncing up and down beneath the weight of them all.

It took them half an hour to reach the village at which
the market was being held, and by the time they got there,
Leonie was aching from head to foot; her teeth jarred
from the backbreaking grind and bump of the jeep, her
face grubby with the fine dust blown up from the road as
they passed, her bottom sore from perching on the edge of
the metal seat.

They pulled up with an earsplitting shriek at the edge
of the market and all climbed out. Leonie's legs almost
gave under her, cramped from sitting in such a confined
space, but she stared with delight at the crowded scene in
front of her as she followed Mtali and Soeur Bernadette
under the trees growing around the village to where, in a
very small space, people milled around heaps of fruit and
meat and dried fish, screaming what sounded like dire
threats at each other as they bargained, black fingers
jabbing and darting, white teeth flashing, eyes rolling in
their heads as they argued.

They stared, of course, she had expected that, but since
she was with Mtali and the nun her presence was accepted
and politely not commented on, apart from the squeaks a
few of the children gave, pointing apprehensive fingers at
her as she passed, hiding their heads against their mothers
in case she turned an evil eye on them. Mtali and the nun
began to buy from the heaps of mangoes and pawpaws
lying on the ground, filling the great sack which Mtali
had brought with him. The market was oddly very like
an English market—mostly local produce; eggs and game,
fish and vegetables, with here and there a trader from one
of the few towns trying to sell more sophisticated wares,
bracelets or knives, bolts of brightly coloured cloth, san-
dals or gym shoes and piles of vivid plastic bowls and

buckets. These were highly popular, Leonie realised, watching them being carried past in triumph.

As they drove back the jeep made even more fuss than it had on the journey earlier, the weight of the food which had been piled into the back dragging the rusting metal nearer to the road and making it even harder to climb the hills which they had rolled down so easily on the way to the market. On one hill the wheels spun uselessly and they began to slide backwards—Mtali switched off the engine and both Leonie and Soeur Bernadette climbed out and helped to push the groaning vehicle over the brow of the hill. From the calm way the nun behaved, Leonie realised it happened every time, and Mtali's grin gave her the distinct impression he was proud of his jeep's difficult behaviour. When they were crawling, smoking viciously, up a hill he would mutter under his breath to it in his own tongue, the tone more admiring than insulting, chiding and nagging it until it managed to puff itself down the other side.

'I hope you have enjoyed yourself,' Soeur Bernadette said as they staggered out of the jeep in the Mission compound, and Leonie laughed and nodded.

'I'll never forget it,' she said drily, rubbing her back with a rueful hand. She followed Mtali into the doctor's bungalow and found her father in the kitchen washing himself at the cracked sink. Staring in surprise at his oily hands and face, she asked: 'Is something wrong?'

He grinned at her. 'Just the generator playing up—nothing unusual, it decides to pack up every once in a while and I'm the only one who knows how to get it going if Mtali isn't here.'

Mtali was gazing gloomily at him and asked something in his own tongue. The doctor nodded and replied, and, as Mtali gave a click of the tongue and vanished, Dr Denis explained to Leonie: 'We saved up for two years to buy a generator—I need it for the hospital, but they cost more than we could afford at first. I had to get a secondhand one and it has a very temperamental character, it works in fits and starts.'

'I wondered how you'd managed to get electricity here. Who did the wiring?'

'Mtali and I did that, with the help of a book I sent for from France.' He dried his hands on a ragged but clean towel and smiled at her. 'Mtali can turn his hand to anything. He has brains and clever fingers.'

Leonie went to her own room to wash and saw the water running red as she rinsed off the soap from her face; the dust from the road had even got into her hair and she would have to wash that when she had her bath. Water was scarce, her father had warned her to use it sparingly, learn to stand in the bath and empty a bucket of cold water over her head. The life they all led was a matter of constant compromise, she was already realising, a permanent battle between human will power and the savagery of nature, the dark threat of the jungle encroaching on them day and night. You could never forget it—it made itself audible, the squeal and screech of invisible animals among the trees, the drone and whirr of insects, the chirruping of birds flying from jungle to compound in search of food. The lack of comfort, the atrocious heat, the humidity, the mosquitoes and snakes—it should all have been intolerable, but Leonie was aware of feeling more alive than she had ever felt in her entire life.

Back in England she led a carefully cherished life in a very comfortable home, her job was easy and well paid, her surroundings beautiful—but looking back she saw herself like a cat on a soft, silk cushion, half asleep from sheer boredom. She hadn't been bored since she arrived here; she had been disturbed, excited, curious, nervous, even alarmed—but never bored.

She found herself settling happily into the pattern of daily life at the Mission, instinctively finding a place for herself there; helping with the routine tasks in the hospital, helping Mtali with the cooking, teaching him new ways of preparing the scrawny chickens or the tough, highly flavoured pork which needed strong spices to make it palatable.

They were all so close—a small family which squabbled cheerfully and affectionately while they got on with the work which bound them all together. The ties binding them were those of respect for each other's abilities and characters, concern and caring for each other and for their patients. Leonie envied them, she longed to become a part of that closely knit family. It was a feeling she had never experienced before. Her mother and stepfather had always treated her as a child, and, when you are expected to behave in a certain way, you do. Leonie had thought and felt as a child until now. Treated as an adult, she slowly began to awake from the half-sleep in which she had been cocooned.

She found herself thinking far too much about Greg Thornton. His image haunted her mind at nights as she lay behind the netting listening to the ceaseless sounds of the jungle. There had been a silent challenge in his eyes. She hadn't understood it, but it had stayed in her mind and it kept her awake at nights. Just to remember the kiss he had given her made her body burn, made her twist and sigh in the stifling heat. Even when she finally fell asleep it was to dream about him and her dreams disturbed her. She often woke up to find him already in her mind, and that worried her, too. She was unable to forget him, however hard she tried.

Two days later she was woken up in the early hours of the morning by the barking of the stray dogs that haunted the Mission compound, their thin-flanked, scrawny bodies often to be seen slinking between the mud houses or scavenging for scraps on the midden to the rear of them where the natives flung their refuse. Leonie had tried to feed them soon after she arrived, but her father had warned her to leave them well alone. They were wild, showed their teeth when she approached, snarling, and their rough, dusty coats carried vermin.

Darkness lay over the compound like a heavy pall, stifling and humid. Leonie sat up, listening with a frown as the dogs yapped. No doubt it was only a villager arriving to ask her father to come and visit someone taken sick in the night, but the disturbance was unusual enough to worry her. The dogs rarely barked.

'Who is it, Mtali?' Leonie heard her father's sleepy voice, heard his movements in the corridor, then loud, harsh voices answered and her father spoke again in the thick native tongue.

Leonie slid out of bed. She found her jeans and pulled them on, dragged a cotton sweater over her head. What was going on? While she was dressing she heard shouting, a crash, scuffling. Outside the bungalow she heard stealthy movements. A gunshot rang out and Leonie heard bare feet running in the dust of the baked earth. She froze, stiffening, then ran to the door and opened it. The corridor was empty except for Mtali, who lay face down on the floor, his arms flung out.

She knelt beside him, turning him over gently. Blood crawled down one side of his temple from a ragged gash.

'Oh, my God,' Leonie whispered, staring at the wound. Had he been shot? Where was her father?

She heard someone moving, the front door of the bungalow opening and closing, and looked round in a mixture of hope and fear, to find Soeur Bernadette hurrying towards her, wearing her habit but bare-headed, startling Leonie, who had never seen the nun without her usual coif, the tight black curls which clung to her head making her look oddly young, vulnerable and more human.

'Leonie!' Soeur Bernadette gasped, stopping at the sight of her. 'Thank God, I was afraid . . .' Her words broke off as she saw Mtali and she knelt quickly to put a hand on his neck, searching for a pulse while her eyes inspected the wound on his temple.

'Has he been shot?' Leonie asked huskily. 'Where's my father? Soeur Bernadette, what's happening? Where's my father?'

The nun did not answer. 'This looks like a blow from a rifle butt to me,' she said instead. 'It isn't serious, I think.'

Mtali's lids flickered and lifted, his black eyes dazed as he stared up at their faces until realisation flashed into his stare and he tried to sit up.

'No, no, lie still, you may have concussion,' Soeur Bernadette said, gently holding him down. 'What happened, Mtali?'

He swallowed, his throat moving in a convulsive way, and began to talk in his own tongue. Leonie couldn't understand what he was saying, but she could read the shock and alarm in Soeur Bernadette's face. The nun listened, nodding, asked some more questions, then looked at Leonie, her dark eyes shining with unshed tears. 'There has been some sort of fighting between the rebels and the government forces thirty miles or so from here—the men who took your father wanted him to attend to their wounded.'

Leonie's mouth was dry with fear. 'Will he be safe? Will they let him go afterwards?'

'I'm sure they will,' the nun assured her. 'He is more use to them alive than dead and he has a very good reputation in Mameea—he is very popular with the people, they won't kill him.' She took Mtali's arm as he raised himself from the floor. 'Take his other arm, Leonie, we must get him to the hospital so that I can stitch that wound.'

Mtali protested, trying to walk alone, but Soeur Bernadette was insistent. Between them they helped him out of the bungalow and into the warm night air, the silence having returned to the compound, although Leonie saw faces peering at them from behind the shelter of the woven mats which hung in front of the windows in smaller mud houses. The wind moved, rustling the palm leaves, and the moon swam slowly out from behind the black web of the forest, lighting their path. The scrawny dogs that hung around the Mission yapped excitedly as the little group made its way to the hospital. Soeur Angélique, fully dressed, with a torch in her hand, was standing at the door waiting for them, and she burst out with tremulous questions in French. Soeur Bernadette's answers only made her more worried and she groaned and sagged against the door.

'We must attend to Mtali,' Soeur Bernadette said to her. *'Venez vite avec moi, ma soeur.'*

In the little office they let Mtali slide into a chair, his body slumped backwards, his skin sweating with pain. The nuns cleaned and stitched the wound, then dressed it with gauze. Leonie looked away as they worked, feeling slightly sick. She was unable to rest, her mind disturbed, anxiety making her nerves jump.

'How does that feel, Mtali?' Soeur Bernadette asked him and he thanked her gravely, fingering his bandage.

'What's going to happen to my father?' Leonie asked,

twisting her fingers into a cat's cradle at her waist. 'Isn't there anything we can do?'

'Yes,' said a voice behind them, and she looked round to find Father Armand there, wearing a shabby old dressing-gown, his slight body trembling as he shuffled towards them.

'Father! What are you doing out of bed! I told you to stay there, there's nothing you can do!'

He leaned on the desk, his brown skin stretched over his bony knuckles. 'I must radio for Joe at once. Leonie must leave as soon as Joe can get here.'

'No!' Leonie cried, shaking her head. 'I can't go without knowing what's happened to my father! He could be dead or wounded, anything could have happened to him.'

'There's nothing you could do whatever has happened to him, you must get out of here. If your father were here, you know he'd insist on it.' Father Armand falteringly made his way to the ancient radio transmitter.

Leonie made a protesting little movement, as if to stop him, and Soeur Bernadette put a hand on her shoulder, smiling at her. 'Father is right, you must leave—go and pack your things. Joe could be here in two hours if he took off at once.'

Father Armand had sat down and was beginning to operate the small old-fashioned set which crackled and fizzed. With a sinking heart, Leonie recognised that she had no real choice. Slowly she turned and went out on to the verandah. Day was breaking, the ground mist from the forest creeping softly between the houses, the flash and call of the birds beginning. She halted, watching a woman roll up the woven mat which hung over her window in one of the tiny mud huts on the far side of the compound. Everything looked so normal, so peaceful, it seemed incredible that only a few miles away there had been fighting and men wounded, if not killed. As she was about to step off the verandah she heard Father Armand saying heavily: 'Joe isn't answering, I'm getting no reply at all.'

Leonie froze and listened, then slowly walked back into the hospital. Across the office the priest looked at her, his face worried.

'Joe didn't answer?' she asked, and he shook his head.

'I wonder whether it would be wisest to keep you here or send you back by road,' he thought aloud. 'Either way I'm taking a risk.'

'It all depends whether the fighting is widespread or just one incident up on the savannah,' Soeur Bernadette suggested. 'If the government have contained it she might get through, but they may have sealed off the roads. She could have trouble getting through and we would have to send someone with her.'

'I will go,' said Father Armand, and the nun looked at his frail face, the perspiration trickling down his sallow skin. She smiled wryly, shaking her head.

'You could not make that journey and we may need you here.' She glanced at Mtali, who said: 'Yes, I go,' getting up, his hand automatically reaching for the back of the chair as he swayed.

'He isn't fit to travel,' Leonie broke out. 'Neither of them are! I shall stay—I may be useful, you may need me.'

'Your father would be very angry,' the nun said, and Leonie gave her a defiant smile.

'Let him be! If Joe can't come to get me, what choice do we have?'

'I'll try Joe again,' said Father Armand, reaching for the headphones of the set, but as he began fiddling with it they all heard the screech of tyres on dry earth and a

vehicle squealing to a halt outside in the compound.
Leonie turned and ran, trembling, with the two nuns right
behind her and Father Armand and Mtali bringing up the
rear. She halted on the verandah, her eyes flying to the
dusty jeep parked outside. Her father was not in it, but Greg
Thornton was, and he was springing out as she looked at
him, moving round the vehicle towards them at a run.

'Thornton!' Father Armand muttered on a note of deep
relief. 'Thank God.' His voice died away as he stared at
the man getting out of the driver's side of the jeep, his
long legs uncoiling stiffly. He was a broad, solid man in
an Army uniform, the peaked cap shading a black face
glistening with sweat.

Greg gave Leonie a brief, penetrating look as he passed
her. Urgently, he asked Father Armand: 'Where's the
doctor?'

Father Armand began to answer in French, his voice
rapid, and Greg's face changed as he listened. He looked
down the steps at the soldier, his hard mouth a straight
line. The other man pushed back his peaked cap and
studied the priest with impassive eyes.

'What now?' Greg asked the man, who shrugged.

'Did the doctor go of his own accord?'

Mtali fingered the bandage over his forehead and
answered in a guttural tone, shaking his head, while the
Army officer watched him without a flicker of expression.
It was impossible to tell if he believed Mtali's story or
not, but then he turned back towards the jeep and Greg
asked: 'Where are you going now?'

'I'll go on to Kissiloga,' the man grunted, climbing back
into the jeep and starting the engine. 'Coming?'

'Wait a moment,' Greg said swiftly. The soldier sighed
and cut the engine, his hands on the wheel, impatience
written all over him.

Greg looked at Leonie. 'You can't stay here now, I told you it was dangerous. The fighting has broken out within a day's march of here. You must come with us, I'll get you on a plane out of here as soon as I can.'

The soldier turned his head and stared at her, asked Greg something in French which Leonie couldn't understand, and Greg answered him, frowning. The soldier muttered a reply, his brows drawn together, his eyes still on Leonie. She heard Father Armand take a shaken breath, felt Soeur Bernadette shift anxiously, move closer to her.

Greg rapped back a reply, his long body tense, and the soldier answered irritably. Leonie looked round at the priest and whispered: 'What are they saying? What's wrong?'

Greg heard her and broke off what he was saying to look at her with fierce grey eyes. 'Major Umulu says they won't let you through to Kissiloga, they would stop you at the first roadblock and arrest you.'

She paled. 'Why?'

'Your father is in the hands of the rebels, the government won't be sure where his loyalties lie and they'll take you as a sort of hostage,' said Greg, his face harsh. The morning sunshine was brightening all around them, making his brown skin gleam, his black hair take on the sheen of polished jet.

Leonie took a long, frightened breath and Greg stared at her with frustrated anger. 'I told you!' he grated, and she bit her inner lip.

'If she stays here?' Father Armand asked, and the Army officer shrugged his broad shoulders.

'She can't stay here,' Greg flung back. He moved restlessly a pace back to the jeep, began to mutter to Umulu in a low voice they couldn't hear. It was obvious from his face, from the face of the other man, that Greg was pleading with him; arguing, protesting, perhaps even trying to bribe him.

The soldier climbed out of his jeep and spoke to Leonie directly, his arrogant face commanding. 'Papers? You have papers?'

'Get them,' Greg ordered, and she gave him an indignant look as she ran back to her father's bungalow to search for the official documents she had brought with her—her passport, her visa, her driving licence. Her hands were trembling and she was very apprehensive as she went back with them. Greg took them from her and handed them to the officer, who looked through them, forehead creased.

He and Greg had another private discussion a few yards away, their voices low, then Greg turned away and came over to where Leonie and the others were standing.

'There's only one faint chance of getting her past the roadblocks and safely to Kissiloga. Umulu says that if she were my wife they'd let her through without question.'

Leonie's head lifted in amazement and shock. Greg was staring at Father Armand fixedly, he didn't look her way at all.

'He suggests you tell them she's your wife?'

Greg grimaced. 'That wouldn't be enough—I'd need proof of it. We need a wedding certificate, documentary proof.'

Father Armand eyed him, a smile beginning on his weatherbeaten face. 'You want me to forge papers claiming she's your wife, you mean?'

Greg nodded. 'You can do it, you have the necessary forms here, don't you? You're authorised to perform weddings and register them.'

'It is a serious offence,' Major Umulu said suddenly, staring at the priest. 'If it was found out you could be executed. The government is very nervous at the moment, they would shoot you first and think about it afterwards.' He looked at Greg. 'My friend, it would be wiser if you really married the girl. A quick service and a certificate, then when you get back to England you can annul the marriage.'

Leonie had turned a bright, scalding pink from her neck to her hairline. 'You can't be serious! I never heard anything so . . .'

'Shut up!' Greg ordered, his eyes flashing in her direction.

Trembling with fury, she hurled back: 'Who do you think you're talking to? You don't really expect me to go through some phoney wedding ceremony with you just to get away from here? I'd rather take my chances with the government.'

'Nobody asked you what you wanted,' Greg informed her angrily. 'If you'd taken my advice and got out two days ago, you wouldn't be causing all this trouble.' He switched his bright, hard eyes back to Father Armand. 'Umulu is right, Father—you would be taking a risk if you forged the papers. Would you be prepared to marry us now? All it would need is a few quick words, just a form, no need to go through the whole rigmarole of a wedding. Just enough for you to be able to claim you really did marry us before you gave us the certificate.'

'No!' Leonie burst out, quivering from head to toe. 'I won't—Father, don't listen to them, the idea is laughable!'

Father Armand fingered his chin thoughtfully and Soeur Bernadette met his eyes, nodding her head.

The Major looked up at the sky, studying the rise of

the sun through the clear blue. 'I'll wait for ten minutes,' he said. 'Then I am leaving, with or without you, Greg.'

'We'll be with you,' Greg told him brusquely, then his fingers fastened around Leonie's slender wrist in a painful grip and he yanked her after him towards the tiny Mission church whose white mud walls gleamed in the sunlight.

She dragged behind him, her toes seeking a purchase in the dry earth, indignantly muttering at him to stop. 'I won't do anything so stupid, the idea is insane—I won't!'

He flung open the door of the church and looked down at her, the steel of his eyes sparking. 'You'll do what I tell you.'

'I won't,' she protested as he pulled her through the door and down the aisle towards the altar whose plain white cloth bore only a vase of local white lilies, their folded cups tongued by long golden pollen-dusted stamens.

Father Armand and the two nuns pursued them and the priest put a white stole around his neck and picked up a missal from the altar rail.

Leonie looked around the shadowy church at where the sunlight trickled like silent water down the walls, feeling like someone in the grip of a crazy dream. 'This is absurd, Father, you can't do it,' she begged, and he frowned, putting a finger between the fluttering pages of the book he held.

'If she is really unwilling, Greg,' he began, but Greg cut in on him tersely.

'She's willing.' He bent down and muttered crisply into Leonie's ear: 'One more out of you and I'll gag you!' He straightened. 'We're ready when you are, Father.'

Leonie listened dazedly as the priest began to hurry through the French service. He stopped and looked at her and Greg's fingers tightened on her wrist. 'Say yes,' he muttered.

'Yes,' Leonie said, and then as her own voice whispered away into the sunlit reaches of the little church wondered if she had really said it.

Two minutes later she watched Father Armand writing out the official certificate of marriage. She and Greg signed it, the two nuns signed it and Father Armand handed it to Greg, who thrust it into his shirt pocket.

'When she is back in England she must seek advice about how to make sure the marriage is not legal,' Father Armand told Greg. 'It will be easy to have it annulled.' He paused, staring at Greg. 'So long, of course, as it has not been consummated.'

'Yes, yes,' Greg agreed. 'Thanks, Father.' He looked down at Leonie. 'Get your money, your flight tickets, anything else you may need, but keep it within reason. We've got to travel light. The sooner we get to Kissiloga the better.'

She still stood there, her mind confused by the rapidity of the events, and he snapped: 'Get going, for God's sake!'

Leonie ran back to the bungalow and got together a bundle of her more essential possessions, coming out again to find Major Umulu in the jeep behind the wheel, drumming his black fingers on the wheel, a look of impatience in his face. Greg stood beside the jeep, his eyes on her as she came back towards them.

Halting, Leonie looked at Father Armand and the nuns, tears coming into her eyes suddenly. 'I can't leave,' she whispered. 'I can't just go not even knowing if he's safe . . .'

'You must,' Soeur Bernadette told her huskily and put both arms around her to kiss her wet cheeks in the French fashion, hugging her briefly.

'*Au revoir*, Leonie,' she said, pushing her towards Greg,

but Leonie hovered, giving Father Armand a pleading look.

'If the hospital has to take in dozens of wounded men you'll need me,' she pointed out. 'You'll need every pair of hands you can get, Father, you know you will.'

'Leonie, your father would never forgive me if I let you stay,' he said. 'Both sides of this quarrel would find you a very useful weapon, don't you understand that? Your father means something to the people here, both sides will want him, and they might try to blackmail him by holding you. Greg's right, you have to get out now, for your father's sake. Don't force a choice like that on him.'

Her face whitened still further and she saw, at last, why they were so insistent that she leave—it wasn't just because they feared for her safety, it was her father's safety they were most concerned about and that left her no choice at all.

'Get in the jeep,' ordered Greg, picking her up in an ungainly huddle and dropping her into the seat. He climbed in beside her, the jeep shot away out of the dusty compound with the dogs barking behind them, and Leonie craned her neck to wave to the little group standing there in the morning light. The last thing she saw was Mtali's tall figure, his black hand raised in a final farewell and tears in his eyes. Mtali loved her father, she had come to realise, and just as the fear for her safety was largely a fear for her father, so Mtali's tears were for Dr Denis, too. She smothered a sob and Greg looked round at her.

'You're a little fool, aren't you?' he said, flicking a finger down her wet cheek.

CHAPTER FIVE

THEY were travelling far too fast for the rough jungle road, the wheels crashing down into potholes from time to time, but running out again, the whole vehicle swaying. Major Umulu drove with maniacal concentration, bent over the wheel as though he were in a race. Leonie eyed his profile nervously. She hoped he wasn't going to drive like this all the way to Kissiloga.

'How long will it take us to get to the airport?' she asked Greg.

'How long would you say, Umulu?' he asked the Major in reply, and over his shoulder, without looking round, the Major grunted: 'Maybe six hours. Depends on whether the roadblocks have been set up.'

'Six hours!' Leonie exclaimed, and Greg turned his head to regard her drily.

'If we're lucky.'

Leonie subsided, her body constantly thrown about by the high speed at which they were moving. At times she grabbed the side of the jeep and hung on, teeth gritted, knowing that Greg was watching her with an amused grin which did nothing to sooth her temper.

'We tried to get hold of Joe,' she said, suddenly remembering that they had never succeeded. 'We couldn't raise him—is he okay, do you know?'

Greg frowned. 'He set me down on the savannah the morning we left the Mission and flew back to Kissiloga. You say you couldn't raise him? That could mean he was flying up country or that his plane had been confiscated.'

'Confiscated?'

'Joe's a free agent, he has dealings with both sides and the government knows it. He used to work for them, but Joe's a bit of a free-wheeler, he wouldn't play the game their way and he set up on his own. They probably suspect him of ferrying supplies out to the rebel tribesmen.'

'Does he?' Leonie asked in whispered surprise, and Umulu turned his head to give her a sudden grin, a flash of white teeth which made her jump. The man so rarely smiled.

Greg seemed amused, too. 'If I knew anything about Joe's business I certainly wouldn't talk about it in front of Umulu—he's a government man.' He grinned at Umulu, who grinned back before returning his attention to the road. Greg looked round at Leonie mockingly. 'Umulu just happens to be a buddy of mine. We go back a long way, don't we, Umulu?'

'A long way,' Umulu agreed without looking round.

'But I don't know anything about Joe's activities,' Greg went on calmly. 'He doesn't tell me and I don't ask. In this part of the world it isn't wise to ask questions.' The statement was deliberately delivered, his eyes warning her. 'In fact, it's very unwise indeed.'

Leonie absorbed that advice in silence. She looked at the tangled jungle between which they were passing and her eyes helplessly misted over with tears—where was her father? Having so recently found him, had she already lost him? She moved restlessly, her body as tense as live wire, shifting on the uncomfortable seat, and Greg shot a hard, perceptive look at her.

'Worried?'

She nodded, unable to speak, and he reached over and took her hand into his own, holding it firmly.

'Your father will be safe enough, he has something both

sides need badly—medical knowledge. The men trust him, he's been living here for so many years now that he's become something of a legend. I can't think of anyone who would hurt him.'

She smiled tremulously at him. 'I hope you're right.' A thought occurred to her and she asked with a frown: 'How did you find out that he was my father?'

Greg's face changed, wry amusement entering it. 'Mtali told me the morning we left the Mission. He overheard me asking Joe some questions and not getting any answers. Joe can clam up like a metal safe when he likes. Mtali decided I ought to know.'

'Oh, did he?' Leonie retorted. 'Why did he think that, I wonder? He has no right to repeat confidential information.'

'Why shouldn't I know?' Greg demanded. 'Are you ashamed of the fact?'

Her face rushed with hot colour. 'Ashamed of my father? Of course not!'

'Then why shouldn't I know about it? Why all the secrecy?'

'My parents were divorced, I hadn't seen my father since I was two. I didn't know if he wanted to be reminded that he had a daughter,' she said. 'And when I got to the Mission it was clear that nobody there knew he had been married and had a child—so I was right not to talk about it until I'd seen him, wasn't I?'

Greg considered that and shrugged. He did not answer and Leonie looked at him indignantly.

'I notice you dislike admitting I could be right,' she pointed out, and he looked at her from under lowered black lashes with a teasing smile but made no effort to argue.

'Why are you going to Kissiloga, anyway?' she asked. 'Are you leaving too?'

He shook his head. 'I have to get some pictures on the plane and then contact the government, get an interview with the President, if I can, then I'll be going back to the savannah.'

Leonie looked away, her skin oddly chill in spite of the ovenlike heat of the morning. She felt Greg watching her and resolutely kept her face turned away from him, giving him only her tender, youthful profile to inspect, hoping it betrayed nothing of the inner turmoil. She was being put on a plane like a child while Greg and her father stayed there with the constant threat of death hovering around them. She was angry and resentful about that, but she was sad, too, because she *was* afraid and she knew it. The idea of being caught up in a vicious civil war terrified her.

It wasn't so much violence or even death that frightened her—it was the unknown, the black shadows of the jungle which could hide *anything*. It is always what you don't know, can't even guess, that frightens you most.

Her own fear made her bitterly angry with Greg because he had seen it, he knew she was scared and out of her depth, which was why he had high-handedly forced her to go through that charade of a marriage with him and come away. He was managing her for her own good, just as Thomas Lincoln had always done, and that made her feel like a puppet, a manipulated doll who could not be allowed to think or act for itself, had to be controlled by someone stronger. If she could have spat back at him, taken control of her own destiny from his hands, she would not feel quite so helplessly bitter. It was because she had to allow him to push her around that she sat there seething with useless resentment. It was bad enough to realise that you were a coward, that you were out of your depth in a situation, but it was far worse to know that someone else saw it so clearly.

The jeep roared on through the jungle, the sun mounting higher all the time through the blue sky. Leonie knew her skin was grimy with yellowy red dust, she could taste it in her mouth, feel it on her jeans as her hands shifted on her knees.

They ran down into a river valley just before noon and found the bridge blocked off, a small band of soldiers guarding it. Major Umulu drew up with a squeal of brakes and got out stiffly to talk to them. They walked round the jeep, kicking the tyres and staring at Greg and Leonie. Major Umulu flung out a hand towards Greg, snapping his fingers in a peremptory way, saying something in the native tongue. Greg handed over his own papers. The young officer in command of the guard looked at them, then looked at Leonie and asked something. Greg produced the marriage certificate and the officer looked at that, nodded and handed it back to him with the other documents. Major Umulu got back into the jeep, the barricade was lifted and they set off across the bridge. There was a village on the far side, a few dozen mud-walled houses dozing in the noonday sun, the narrow street empty except for a few dogs which lifted up their heads as the jeep rattled by and barked without bothering to move.

'I'm thirsty,' Leonie said in a defiant voice, and Major Umulu looked round at her, braking. He gave Greg a questioning look and got back a nod.

'So am I,' Greg admitted ruefully.

'Yeah, me too,' Major Umulu grinned, and began to reverse back into the little square which was the hub of the village. The dogs lumbered to their feet, yapping and snarling, the mats hanging over doors and windows were twitched aside and dark faces peered out at them. Major

Umulu stopped the jeep and climbed out with Greg and Leonie close behind him. He looked around the village and a very large woman in a gaudy wrap-around sarong of multi-coloured cotton appeared in a doorway, staring towards them, her black eyes wary.

Umulu set off in her direction, speaking in the native tongue and getting a smiling reply.

'The local equivalent of a pub,' Greg said to Leonie in a cheerful voice. 'She just told Umulu that she brewed corn beer and would sell us some.'

Leonie looked aghast. 'Corn beer? I don't drink beer.'

'When you're thirsty you drink anything—and you are certainly not drinking the water, the local stuff is loaded with germs. Corn beer's a pretty safe beverage, the distilling process kills all known germs.'

The dark, stuffy little room into which they walked smelt strongly of brewing and Leonie felt sick as the odour hit her nostrils. Greg glanced at her and gave a sigh.

'We'll drink our beer outside in the shade of the trees,' he told Umulu, who was engaged in a noisy flirtation with the lady proprietor.

'Okay, suit yourself,' said Umulu without looking at him, and Greg looked amused.

'He's a ladykiller, he told Leonie, and Umulu laughed, throwing him a brief glance.

'Hey, man, isn't that the pot calling the kettle black?'

'If the cap fits,' Greg grinned and Umulu roared with loud amusement.

The owner of the house handed Greg two large earthenware mugs which he carried carefully back into the village square. Leonie looked around for a safe place to sit down, but the dry earth was alive with ants and she had already learnt that their bite could be vicious. Greg surveyed her. 'Hang on,' he said, and went back into the house again after handing her the two mugs. He returned with a folding stool of native origin, the legs beautifully carved, the seat of strong but faded brown webbing.

Greg placed it just inside the shadow of a eucalyptus and Leonie sat down gingerly. 'Thank you,' she said, offering him his mug of beer. She could feel people staring from every house, but no faces showed at the doors. Even the dogs kept their distance, watching them with lowered heads like bulls getting ready to charge.

Greg lounged there, swallowing his beer with narrowed eyes on the village. Leonie saw a trickle of perspiration running down his brown throat as he swallowed. His skin had the sheen of polished wood, the black hair in dramatic contrast to his light grey eyes and while he was not aware of it Leonie stared at him and felt again that strange burning ache inside her. As he lifted his mug to his lips the muscles of arm and shoulder visibly rippled under his dusty shirt, the open collar giving her a glimpse of his smooth tanned skin, the line of bone where his throat hollowed out. While she watched he put a hand to his shirt, unbuttoning another few inches to let the air reach his sweating skin.

'God, I'm hot,' he muttered, and the sound of his voice made her jump. She had been totally engrossed in staring, absorbing every detail of how he looked, and she blinked, her nerves prickling.

As if aware suddenly that she had been staring he turned his head and their eyes met. Leonie felt her face washed with abrupt colour and Greg registered her blush with intent observation. To cover her confusion, she asked hastily: 'Why is Major Umulu going to Kissiloga?'

'How many times do I have to tell you—don't ask questions,' Greg told her. 'And finish your beer.'

'It's sour,' Leonie complained and he leaned towards

her with barely parted lips to say softly: 'Drink it.'

'Stop pushing me around!' she flared, then caught the hard glint of those metallic eyes and lowered her head to take another, reluctant sip of the cloudy liquid. She was sweating at every pore and her throat was as dry as a kiln. Taking a deep breath, she tilted the mug and let the contents run down her throat, shuddering as she swallowed. As the beer entered her bloodstream she felt a new wave of perspiration breaking over her body, but at least her mouth no long felt like the inside of an oven.

When the mug was empty she set it down on the ground and Greg gave her a grin. 'Feel better?'

She nodded, looking round at the open door through which she could see Major Umulu laughing as he flirted with the owner. 'What do I do about this phoney marriage when I get back to England?' she asked Greg. 'Should I take the certificate to a solicitor?'

'No need,' Greg said drily. 'We were never married, the certificate is a fraud—do you have to have everything spelled out for you? Father Armand didn't really marry us, he just went through some of the motions. If he hadn't, he could have been in trouble if the government chose to take umbrage about it. We have a piece of paper and Father Armand is in the clear, that's all. Once you're on the plane to England, you can tear it up with impunity and just forget the whole thing.'

'He didn't really marry us?' Leonie thought back to the brief ceremony in the church, almost smelling the heavy scent of the lilies again. 'But . . .'

'He didn't marry us,' Greg cut in tersely. 'Get that through your head—we aren't married, we just have a bit of paper which says we are.' He hurled a derisive look at her which swept from her dusty blonde curls to her feet. 'So you can stop worrying about what your unofficial fiancé says when he hears—there's no damned reason why he should ever know, unless you choose to tell him.'

She bristled crossly and stood up, her head just reaching his wide shoulder and making her feel even more resentfully aware of his superior masculine strength. 'I'm not worrying about what Oliver will say!'

'Oliver!' he repeated scathingly. 'God help us—what a name! What does he do, this Oliver?'

'He's a director of my father's firm,' she said, then caught his glance and added impatiently: 'My stepfather's firm—Oliver's father is a partner, he and my stepfather founded the firm together.'

'And you're going to marry this guy? How cosy,' Greg mocked icily. 'Whose idea was that? It sounds to me like a take-over bid rather than a marriage.'

'You know nothing about it! You've never even met Oliver, what right do you have to make remarks like that?'

'As your temporary if slightly phoney husband, I'd say I had a perfect right to comment on who's going to follow in my footsteps,' he said, and laughed, making her fizz with shaking temper.

'Oliver won't be following in your footsteps,' she threw back, and his smile vanished, his lips straightening into a fierce, menacing line.

'Dead right he won't,' he said tersely. 'I don't know why I'm involved with you at all. Hell, I must be crazy! I've got enough problems without adding a blue-eyed blonde to them, especially one who doesn't even know she's born yet.'

Major Umulu came out of the house, shouting back some lively remark to the owner and strode towards them, smiling. 'Ready?' he asked Greg, who gave a curt nod.

'Ready is right,' he said, and turned towards the jeep,

his long legs covering the dusty road so fast that Major Umulu stared after him and then gave Leonie a thought-ful, curious look before he followed.

They drove out of the village accompanied by a pack of the thin, yelping dogs who pursued the jeep until they accelerated beyond the last house. Leonie looked back to see the dogs crouched, panting, in triumph by the road-side, apparently under the firm impression that they had driven the intruders away. She looked back and watched the dust blowing up around the wheels, wondering how long it would take them now to reach the airport. Did Major Umulu realise that the marriage was a lie? Clearly he and Greg were close friends—possibly the Major was perfectly well aware that the whole thing was a charade, but he had stayed out of the church, taken no part in the performance, so that no responsibility for it lay with him. All he had to do was say that he had been in the village when they were married—he would not need to say he had been present at the service.

Twenty miles on, they were stopped at another road-block by a very surly group of soldiers who made all three of them get out at gunpoint. Major Umulu began to bark at them, his face frowning. He beckoned to Greg, who produced the sheaf of documents again and, while they were involved in an argument with the heavily built man in command, the other men stood and stared at Leonie, their rifles levelled at her in a way that made the back of her neck tingle with fear.

One of the men took a step nearer and put out a hand to her windblown blonde curls, grinning. She flinched as his fingers took hold of a thick cluster of hair and the other men chuckled. Leonie lifted her chin, trying not to show how frightened she was, and Greg shot a swift glance in her direction, spinning as he saw what was going on.

Major Umulu grabbed his arm, muttering inaudibly under his breath. Leonie heard Greg's breath hissing through his teeth, saw the vibrating rage in the tension of his body. Major Umulu released him and walked over towards the spot where the soldiers ringed Leonie. He rapped out a string of harsh words and the little group slouched back, their expressions sullen.

Greg came over and got into the jeep. Major Umulu gestured to Leonie to do so, too, and then he got behind the wheel. The jeep throbbed as the engine started. The soldiers lifted the barricade and the jeep drove past them with Leonie staring straight ahead of her, trembling, her hands clenched in her lap.

'That's why you had to have an escort,' Greg muttered through closed lips, the words only just comprehensible.

She couldn't answer, she couldn't have managed to utter a word to save her life. Major Umulu and Greg talked beside her while she sat and felt sick with fear, despising herself because she had not even been able to face the implicit threat in the way the soldiers looked at her, she had been petrified. It wasn't so much that one of them had fingered her hair, smiling in that nerve-racking way, as that their eyes had been stripping her all the time she stood there and she had known that if she had not been with Major Umulu and Greg she would have had no chance of dealing with them. Nothing had happened, yet she was ice cold and trembling at what she knew could have happened.

The incident had unnerved her to such an extent that she closed her eyes as the heat of the day wore on, intensifying until she felt it beating down on her neck and face, her ears clanging with the sound of her own overheated blood as though someone was banging a brazen gong inside her head. She half slept, her head dropping sideways towards Greg, and he put an arm round her to support her, letting her heavy head fall on his shoulder. Leonie jerked awake for a second or two, looked up cloudily at him and met expressionless grey eyes, then closed her own eyes in defence and let herself drift back into that empty doze. Under her cheek his shirt was gritty with the dust of the road, but through the thin material she felt the warmth of his skin and the hardness of muscle and bone beneath that. Her whole body sagged towards him, involuntarily seeking that strength, her knee pressed against his, her limbs curled up against him, the security of his touch allowing her to fall into a deep, dreamless sleep.

When she woke up they were still on the move, but now they were much nearer to the coast, the air cooler and less sultry, the roads far better and the villages much closer together. The forests were still spread on either side, but now the trees were vast, towering objects well spaced out and carefully tended—the mahogany trees which were a major source of income for the small country.

Leonie sat up and moved away from Greg, very flushed under his dry glance. He said nothing, but his grey eyes were very vocal, she preferred to pretend not to understand what they were saying.

It was another hour before they reached the perimeter of the airport and ran into another roadblock. Major Umulu was treated with great respect here and they passed without any difficulty, turning through rusty metal gates into the dusty car park.

Major Umulu escorted them both into the flat-roofed airport building which was guarded by soldiers armed with modern rifles. Most of the weapons they had seen today had been ancient objects, some of them even appearing to be left over from the First World War, but now that they were back in territory firmly in control of the government they were meeting well-armed, well-disciplined forces.

Major Umulu strode over to the reception desk and spoke to the man behind it, gesturing to Leonie. After a few moments he came back and said: 'There is a flight out in two hours—plenty of seats free.'

'Will they let her go?' Greg asked, and Major Umulu nodded.

Greg gave a long sigh of relief. Major Umulu said: 'Give me her air ticket and her documents and I'll clear her through myself, it will be safer, make sure there are no awkward questions.'

'Thanks, Umulu,' said Greg, touching his arm briefly. He handed over the sheaf of documents and the Major walked back to the desk with them. Leonie stood staring around the airport, which was much busier than it had been on the day she arrived—there were crowds of people waiting to catch a plane out of Mameea, obviously in flight from the threatened civil war. Every available seat was taken, people walked to and fro with abstracted, anxious faces, their faces dewed with sweat in the stifling heat. While she watched a flight was called and numbers of people surged towards the barriers. She looked at Greg in question and he said: 'That flight is to Johannesburg.'

She nodded, realising that she would be flying via Cairo, as she had come that way. She had meant to spend a week in Egypt on her way back, visiting the famous tourist spots along the Nile, but she no longer felt in the mood for that. Her mind was too disturbed, she couldn't even contemplate the idea of wandering around the pyramids and temples in the Egyptian sunshine while her whole attention was given, instead, to what was happening back here in Mameea.

Major Umulu came back and handed her a small blue card. 'That's your boarding pass,' he said, and she thanked him.

'I'm very grateful for all you've done, Major,' she added, offering him her hand, her eyes shy.

He shook hands, brushing her gratitude away. 'Not at all,' he told her, giving her a brief smile. 'I admire your father very much, he is a marvellous man. I'm glad to have been able to help his daughter.' He turned to say to Greg: 'I'll be on my way—I'll see you later, pick you up at the Ministry tomorrow morning at nine. Don't be late, I won't wait.'

Greg nodded agreement and the Major adjusted his peaked cap, brushed down his uniform and said politely: 'Goodbye, Miss Denis,' before he turned and walked away.

It was the first time Leonie had ever been addressed by her father's name—she had always used her stepfather's surname, and for a moment she felt a sense of shock, a confusion inside herself. Wasn't that what had brought her all this way to a remote African state, though? A sense of uncertainty about herself, about her roots and her background? She stared after the Major dumbly and was still unsure, still in a state of unsettled doubt. Had she learnt anything from this brief visit other than that Mameea was a dangerous place where she did not belong?

'Don't lose that boarding card,' Greg instructed, and she came back to a realisation of her surroundings, her gaze moving back to him.

'I won't, I'm not stupid,' she muttered impatiently.

'Put it somewhere safe,' Greg ordered, handing her back the documents which Major Umulu had handed him. 'Don't lose these, either, you may be booked on this flight, but you'll still need your passport and visa.'

'Would you please stop talking to me as though I was halfwitted? I got myself safely here and I'll get myself safely back!'

'And stay there this time,' Greg bit out. 'Stay where you belong, Goldilocks, keep out of the forest in future. Next time there may not be anyone around to save you from the wild animals.' His eyes mocked her coldly. 'You could have been gobbled up if I hadn't been around to get you out of trouble.'

'Thank you,' she said stiffly, very flushed. 'I realise I owe you . . .'

He interrupted in a low, fierce voice: 'You owe me nothing! I got you out for your father's sake, he would have worried himself sick knowing you were marooned in the middle of a tribal war.'

Leonie looked down, biting her lip. 'Will you let me know if you have any news of him? I'll give you my address, I'll be flying straight back there. Could you cable me as soon as there's word?'

'Yes,' he said shortly. 'Give me the address.'

She scribbled it on a piece of paper and he read it, folded it into a neat square with careful deliberation and tucked it away into his shirt pocket.

'I'm sure he'll be okay,' he said roughly. 'You mustn't worry about him. He's been through worse situations than this, remember. Your father is used to this country. *He* belongs here.'

She lifted her head, very pale now. 'There's no need to keep rubbing it in—you've made your point, stop hammering it into me.'

His face was as tensely controlled as hers, they stared at each other like enemies and deep inside Leonie's body that ache was throbbing with bitter intensity.

All around them people were drifting restlessly, waiting for planes, nervously waiting for news, perhaps, talking in low voices to each other while airport officials walked among them, their faces absorbed as they tried to cope with the sudden panic which was turning the quiet little airport into a sea of worried humanity. Leonie was scarcely aware of them, though. She was aware of nothing but the tall, wide-shouldered man beside her, whose hard-bitten eyes and cynical mouth held an emotion she couldn't quite decipher but which she suspected to lie between anger and contempt. In Greg Thornton's eyes she was a human failure, a product of a way of life he despised.

He let his gaze move down over her slender, dishevelled figure in the shirt and jeans which were stained by hours of travel on dusty roads; damp with perspiration, clinging to her moist skin and making all too clear the feminine curves underneath them. She trembled like a leaf under his slow, evaluating stare, her colour washing back and forth, now hot, now cold.

Greg lifted his eyes to her face again, staring at the vulnerable curve of her mouth. He took a step and Leonie moved at the same instant, her mind blank of thought, driven by an instinct she obeyed without question, the deep ache inside her intensifying to an unbearable level. She stood on tiptoe, Greg's hands gripping her arms, and their mouths met fiercely, hungrily. It was only as his lips touched hers that she knew that the painful nagging ache inside her had been a constant reminder that she needed to touch him, be as close to him as humanly possible. Her body arched against him, she clung, shivering, because she would never again know what it felt like to feel like this, to be in his arms and able to satisfy this intense need.

Suddenly Greg pushed her away, held her at arm's

length and looked at her grimly. 'Get on that plane and don't come back,' he said thickly.

She swallowed, very pale. Behind her she heard the muffled voice of the airport announcer and the rush of people making their way to the boarding gate.

'That's you,' said Greg. 'On your way.'

She turned and walked obediently, jostled by the crowd, almost knocked off her feet as she was thrust by those behind her through the narrow metal gate. She tried to halt, to look back, but the oncoming passengers gave her no chance. She was borne helplessly in the middle of an agitated throng until the airport lounge was out of sight.

Half an hour later the plane lifted off the ground and she looked down as they circled the airport, wondering if Greg had already gone or was still down there somewhere watching her fly away. Tears stung behind her lids as she turned her head away.

CHAPTER SIX

LEONIE spent the night at a hotel in Cairo between planes and woke up in the velvety darkness to find that she had kicked off the thin sheet and lay naked, her skin damp with perspiration after a deep sleep, her mind beset with painful thoughts of Greg. She couldn't remember what she had dreamed about, but she knew those dreams had been of him. With a groan, she sat up and switched on the bedside lamp. The room was furnished in a heavy, ornate fashion from the Edwardian era—dark red plush curtains, close-woven carpets with Eastern patterns of birds and leaf tendrils transformed into geometric blocks of faded colour, a wardrobe and dressing-table of warm, carved wood with a deep, interior gleam, as though years of patient polishing had built up the shine on them.

She heard the hoarse, haunting cry of a muezzin somewhere nearby, the call floating out over the rooftops of Cairo, the busy night-time city which, like all cities, did not become still and empty when darkness fell, but turned instead from work to a search for pleasure. Leonie opened the shutters and stood on the balcony, staring down into the street. The hot, spicy scents of the city floated up towards her, the sky was a star-pricked purple banner flaunting behind the dark outlines of the buildings.

The atmosphere was heavy with romance, it soaked into her mind, making her ache and yearn for something intangible, something she refused to think about. What is the matter with me? she asked herself, turning back into the room, as though hoping to leave behind in the Cairo night scene the feelings which were troubling the surface of her mind, but they came with her as she climbed back into bed. She switched off the light again and the darkness was dancing with images of Greg Thornton, her body was pulsing with the feeling of his mouth moving against her own.

She arrived at the airport next day to be met with a cable which had been delivered an hour earlier. Leonie tore it open with shaking hands, her nerves leaping. It was from Greg and she had to read it twice before she believed it. Her father was safely back at the Mission. He had been released by the rebels and was unharmed.

Leonie was so relieved that she felt sick. The dark-skinned girl at the enquiries desk looked at her questioningly. 'Is anything wrong, miss?'

'No, thank you,' Leonie said huskily, and gave her a strained little smile before she turned and walked away, on legs which had become weak and threatened to give under her at any minute.

She drank some very strong Egyptian coffee thick with sugar while she waited for her plane. She was scarcely aware of the people moving around her. At any other time she would have been fascinated and intrigued by the different languages and garments, the strangeness of her surroundings, but today she had no attention for anything but relief that her father was safe.

She had sent a cable to her stepfather from Cairo, telling him what time she would arrive, and when they landed at Heathrow in grey London drizzle, she walked through the barrier to find him waiting for her, hunched like an angry bear in a thick fawn overcoat, his brows scowling. He looked sulky and sweet, and Leonie ran to hug him, starting to laugh.

He held her away by her shoulders and looked into her

face. 'Do you know what I've been going through?' he demanded in a voice which carried all over the airport terminal and made people in all directions turn their heads to stare. 'Do you know how worried I've been? I didn't know if you were alive or dead. It didn't enter your head that I'd be worried, I suppose? I woke up to hear that there was some sort of civil war in Mameea and I couldn't get any news of you. I rang everyone I could think of, from the Foreign Office to the newspapers, and couldn't find out a thing. Couldn't you have telephoned?'

'There wasn't a phone,' Leonie said, looking at him anxiously. 'I'm sorry if you've been worried.'

'You're sorry! That's supposed to make me feel better, is it?' Thomas Lincoln was a very large man, solidly built with a leonine head of grey hair which had once been a dark brown. His features were all built on the massive scale, his jaw and forehead both conveying a sense of drive and power. He liked his own way and he had a low frustration level which made him burn with angry impatience when anyone opposed him. Despite his anxiety for Leonie's safety, now that she was back he was determined to make his anger plain to her—she had gone against his wishes and Thomas Lincoln wasn't forgetting it. The way he glared at her made that clear.

'I sent you a cable as soon as I reached Cairo!' In fact, she wasn't telling the exact truth, of course, because she had been too tired to think of sending a cable until the next day and had only just remembered then, while she was eating her breakfast.

He grabbed her overnight bag, stared at it, and looked at her. 'Where's your luggage?'

'I had to leave it behind.'

He smouldered with fury, his jaw working. 'Leave it behind? I suppose that means you had to get out of the country in such a hurry that you couldn't wait to pack. Good God—good God!' He stopped roaring simply because he was too angry to speak, his face almost purple with temper.

Leonie put her hand through his arm and smiled at him soothingly. 'Daddy, don't get so upset, you're working yourself up into exploding. I'm safe now and that's all that matters.'

He growled and set off at a stamping pace for the exit with Leonie almost running alongside him. She shivered as they came out into the dull, rainy evening, the street lamps making blurred yellow patterns on the wet pavements and the taxis driving past with a hiss as their tyres skidded on the road. Mameea seemed a million light years away, she found it hard to remember what it felt like to swelter in that tropical heat and feel the red eye of the sun boring an aching hole through your head.

She was thrust like a naughty child into her stepfather's car and he climbed in beside her, slamming his door before he looked round at her and irritably told her: 'Fasten your seat-belt, how many times do I have to tell you that?'

Leonie fastened it, wry humour in her face. She was home and on the surface nothing had changed—Thomas Lincoln still treated her like a halfwitted schoolgirl without a mind of her own and she had no idea how she was ever going to convince him otherwise—but she meant to try.

'How's Oliver?' she asked, and got a sharp look.

'He's fine, not that that really matters to you. You didn't write or ring him, either, did you?'

'I was only away for just over a week! Anyone would think I'd been gone a hundred years!'

'You must have known we would be worried about

you. You knew we didn't want you to go.'

'Yes, I knew,' she said quietly, looking down. 'We went through all this before I went away. I had to go to find out what sort of man my father really was, I explained that to you, can't you try to understand?'

Thomas Lincoln was silent for a moment, his fingers drumming out a hard, irritable rhythm on the wheel, then he said brusquely: 'So you went. Did you find out what you wanted to know?'

Leonie nodded and looked up. 'He told me the truth, Daddy.' She was using the old childhood name deliberately, trying to get home to him that her feelings for him hadn't really changed, he would always be the man who had been her father for as long as she could remember.

She saw a red stain washing up his face. Roughly, he said: 'What did he say about your mother? If he told you lies about her . . .'

'I'm sure he didn't,' Leonie broke in quickly. 'I think he told me the truth. He doesn't blame her, he made it clear that he knew she couldn't help falling in love with you, it was just one of those things.'

Her stepfather stared at her fixedly, that angry flush lying along his cheekbones. 'He told you that? What did he say?'

'He said that she never really loved him the way he loved her, that he went away because he had to realise she was in love with you.' Leonie looked at him directly, their eyes meeting, and said gently: 'That's true, isn't it? That is why he left, he didn't walk out on her at all. She was already in love with you.'

Thomas Lincoln looked away. After a moment, he nodded, but he didn't speak.

'Why didn't you tell me the truth?' Leonie asked, feeling angry. 'Why put all the blame on him like that? I can't understand how you could do it, how you could go on lying to me about him.'

'Your mother was afraid you would despise her,' he muttered. 'And I suppose I was afraid you'd despise me. We didn't expect him to come back into our lives. We wanted to bury him, forget about him.'

'You felt guilty about stealing Mother from him?'

He shifted, embarrassed and irritable. 'I had no reason to feel guilty!' His voice was harsh and uneasy. 'I loved her and she loved me. Why should either of us feel guilty?'

'But you did?' she pressed. 'Otherwise why should you lie about it? Why would you be afraid I'd despise you?'

Thomas sat staring at the rain trickling down the windscreen. 'He's managed to turn you against me, hasn't he? I knew he would, if you went there and talked to him. We were happy, why did you have to go and spoil it?'

'We weren't happy,' Leonie said firmly. 'At least, I wasn't, because it was all a lie, all the stories you told me about him, and you can't build your life on a lie. Now I know the truth and I feel much happier.'

Thomas breathed carefully, frowning. 'What are you going to do now?'

'I don't know,' Leonie said. She put a hand on his on the wheel and he stared at it, his face disturbed, close to tears. 'Why couldn't you have trusted me, Daddy? If you'd told me the truth, I'd have understood. None of you was to blame, I can see that now. I know you loved my mother, I know how happy the two of you were, couldn't you have told me how it really was, and let me make up my own mind about it?'

'You're all I have,' he said, his head bent. 'I didn't dare risk losing you.'

'You're not going to lose me, silly,' she said, and kissed him. Drawing away, she added: 'I'm starving, can we get home and have a meal? I'd forgotten how cold London can be in the summer.'

Thomas took a long, deep breath and started the engine. As he drove his face slowly cleared of the doubt and distress which had briefly shadowed it. They were emotions Thomas Lincoln found uneasy companions and he was eager to be rid of them as soon as possible.

He was a man who shored his life up with walls of self-confidence, assertion, and for a few moments Leonie had seen him with those walls down, self-doubt in every line of his powerful body. This was what he had wanted to hide from her, as he wanted to hide it from himself—he didn't want anyone knowing that he wasn't entirely certain he was always right. Leonie found that realising so much had made her love him more, made him human enough to be loved as nothing else ever had. She had always loved him because all her life he had been her father; omnipotent, omniscient, a granite edifice on the horizon of her life, but it is only when someone is human that you can really love them. You can't love someone who is on another plane altogether, you are always in the weaker position.

As if he were appealing to her he muttered suddenly: 'We only did it because we loved you; that's why we lied.'

She turned her head to smile lovingly at him. 'I know, I do understand.'

He threw her a strangely puzzled, disconcerted look. 'I'm glad you're home safely,' was all he said, but his face showed other thoughts. Leonie had changed. That one week away had altered her, but in a sense the change had been going on underneath for a long time without showing. That was why she had insisted on going to Mameea to find her real father. She had known inside herself that she was growing up, becoming more of a mature woman than a child, but Thomas was refusing to let her grow up, he was trying to keep her a child, because only if she stayed a child could he continue to manipulate and control her.

He needed to feel she was his possession, always in his control, because that helped him to maintain his own sense of himself. He believed that power was force, he wasn't prepared to consider freedom as an alternative. Leonie hadn't been able to grow naturally into an adult, the overbearing shadow of his personality had refused to let her. She had had to walk out of that shadow to find herself.

The rain cleared as they came within sight of their home. The sun peered warily round a cloud and put a finger out, the thin ray of light sliding down over the peaceful green landscape of the countryside beyond London. A rainbow arched across the fields, shimmering briefly before it faded.

'Tell me about the fighting, did you run into any trouble?' her stepfather asked, as though that had just occurred to him.

He turned into the gate and listened as he parked the car outside the house while Leonie poured out the story of what had happened. She carefully left out the details about her mock marriage to Greg Thornton, but she said enough about Greg to make her stepfather very curious.

'What sort of guy was this Greg Thornton?' he demanded as they got out of the car.

'You'd probably like him,' Leonie said, her tone ironic.

He stared at her. 'But you didn't?'

'He pushed me around,' she said, walking to the door. One of the decisions she had made on the long flight to

London was about Greg Thornton—she was going to forget she ever met him as soon as she could and she didn't want to talk about him any more. You can't forget someone if you're always talking about them.

Her stepfather caught her up as she reached the door. 'How much did you see of him while you were there?' he asked suspiciously, staring at her averted face. 'You say his name every other word.'

'Do I?' she asked with pretended surprise, feeling herself flush, then the door opened and there was Oliver, smiling uncertainly at her, and she flung her arms round him to kiss him. Whatever had happened, whatever had changed, one thing would never change. She had known Oliver all her life and she cared for him very much. He might be trying to push her around the way her stepfather had always done, but he was still Oliver and she loved him.

He held her close, laughing. 'Are you trying to get round me?' he asked, kissing her back with enthusiasm.

'I'm just glad to see you again, aren't you glad to see me?' she asked disingenuously, smiling.

'Yes, I suppose I am,' he admitted, his manner reluctant. Leonie had refused to listen to him when he told her not to go to find her real father and Oliver was standing on his dignity. Like her stepfather, he wanted her to let him dictate what she did, what she thought, he didn't want her thinking for herself, that was dangerous. It was dangerous to Oliver because it took her out of his possession. It made her a woman with a mind of her own and a will of her own. That subtracted from Oliver's sense of himself, it diminished him in his own eyes.

'You ran into trouble,' he pointed out. 'I told you it was a foolhardy idea to go to a place like that.'

'So you did,' she agreed cheerfully. 'But here I am—in

one piece, I survived it and I'm back safely.'

'By the skin of your teeth,' her stepfather said accusingly, looking at Oliver. 'Wait till you hear the whole story! She was lucky to get out when she did. I shudder to think what could have happened to her.'

Oliver frowned, his firm-featured face worried. 'What did happen?' he asked her, and Leonie sighed.

'I'm tired, Oliver, I've had a very long day, can't we leave it for tonight? I'm ravenous, and when I've eaten I'm going to have a warm bath and go to bed to sleep for a couple of days. Travelling is exhausting, particularly travelling by air, you spend so many hours just sitting about in airports waiting for planes that show no signs of arriving.'

'Don't try to change the subject,' said Oliver, not fooled by this sudden rush of words.

She walked into the sitting-room and flung herself down into one of the comfortably upholstered chairs with a long sigh. The room looked just the same, furnished in a traditional English fashion, with brocade curtains and chintz-covered sofa and armchairs, the cream-coloured carpet deep and smooth. A lantern-cased clock ticked soberly on the mantelpiece and on the pale apple green walls hung some sporting prints so familiar to her that she barely noticed them except to realise that they were there.

Oliver sat down opposite her in another chair, his hands on his knees, staring at her. He was wearing a dark lounge suit, a city shirt with red stripes and a dark wine tie whose silky weave was picked out with tiny symbols of some club to which he belonged. Oliver was very attractive, his hair a pale brown, his eyes hazel, his skin smooth and closely shaven.

'I want to hear what happened,' he said firmly, and with a faint sigh she began to tell him what she had told her stepfather. When she had faltered to a stop, Oliver frowned angrily.

'You could have been killed—or worse!'

'Is anything worse?' she asked, laughing.

'You know what I mean,' he said, going red and looking at her pointedly, and she did know, of course. Oliver was right—the moment when those soldiers stood around her with their guns pointed at her had made her realise how weak and vulnerable she was, but she knew better than to admit that to Oliver, because he already believed that women were the weaker sex and he would make capital out of her admission.

'Well, I hope you're satisfied now,' he said crossly. 'You've met your father, but I can't see that you've learnt much. After all, it happened nearly twenty years ago, it has nothing to do with today. Why dig up the past? It seems morbid to me.'

'I needed to know,' Leonie said, realising that she would never convince him. Oliver liked life the way it was—he did not want any changes. There had been a comfortable situation between them until now, but she had altered the balance by making a decision of her own, and Oliver was uneasy about it.

'Maybe now you can put it all behind you,' he said challengingly. 'You know what I think? You're restless. It's time we were married, then you'll have plenty to think about. What's the point of waiting? If you still love me, that is . . .' He looked at her hard, a frown creasing his forehead, and she knew her stepfather was watching, too. She knew at once that they had discussed this—that they had both decided to fix a wedding day and make it soon. Her bolt to Africa had alarmed them. Their plans about the future had been laid long ago. Oliver had grown up imitating Thomas Lincoln, following in his footsteps with the expectation of owning the firm one day and Leonie with it. Nothing must interfere with their plans.

She thought about the people she had left behind in Mameea. She had walked into their busy, engrossed lives and walked out again, all in a few brief days. She might never see any of them again, but their impact on her had been like the detonation of a bomb—she knew she would never be the same again, her old life had been blown to shreds and she had to build a new one.

'Do you?' Oliver asked, startling her. She looked at him and saw hurt in his eyes. 'Do you still love me, Leonie? You didn't meet anyone else in Africa, did you?'

'No, of course not,' she said quickly, and was at once aware that she was lying, but she had to soothe away the hurt in Oliver's eyes. Her old affection for him remained, she could not bear to see him look like that.

'Then we'll get engaged right away and fix a wedding date,' Oliver said with a smile, glancing at Thomas Lincoln for approval, which he received at once.

'I think that's a very good idea,' her stepfather said, as though it had only just occurred to him. They both looked at Leonie, who couldn't force herself to speak. Her mind was in absolute turmoil. What was she to do?

She scarcely knew Greg Thornton, she had only spent a couple of days in his company, she knew almost nothing about him. She had known Oliver all her life and she knew she loved him. She had grown up with him, she knew him almost as well as she knew herself, at least on the surface. No doubt Oliver had a private life of his own inside his head, of which she could guess nothing, but she knew more about him than most wives ever knew about their husbands. It was ridiculous to hesitate about marrying him, after all—she would never see Greg Thornton again, and even if she did, he was the last man in the world she would want to marry, because he was worse than Oliver and her stepfather, he would override and domineer, refuse to let her make her own decisions, just as he had refused when he rushed her through that ridiculous charade of a wedding.

'Then what's the problem?' Oliver insisted, and Leonie looked at him and sighed.

'There isn't any problem, I just wanted a week or so to make up my mind.'

'I'll make it up for you,' Oliver told her with a happy smile, and she didn't have the heart to contradict that statement because it made him feel good to say it. 'We'll get engaged right away,' he said, and Leonie said meekly: 'Yes, Oliver.'

That made him look even happier. Life was returning to normal. Oliver was getting his own way, Leonie was behaving the way he wanted her to behave. Her week in Africa could be forgotten along with everything else which threatened Oliver's comfortable, secure existence.

They chose the ring the next day, a beautiful sapphire which glinted an electric, dazzling blue whenever she moved her hand. Leonie kept looking at it with a sense of nervous alarm at finding it on her finger. She was being rushed into a marriage she knew she did not want, but old ties of affection and loyalty bound her and she did not know how to break them.

'Beautiful,' her stepfather said when they showed it to him, but Leonie felt it was not the ring he was talking about. The ring was a symbol of the fact that she was safely engaged to Oliver and their plans for the future were going to go ahead unhindered. They both loved her in their own way and they would have been aghast if she had suggested to them that her happiness was not the paramount idea in their heads, but it was an essential part of their planning that Leonie should be married to Oliver.

'Will there be time to make all the arrangements by around October?' Oliver asked, and Thomas rubbed his chin with one hand while he considered the matter.

'I don't see why not.'

'I'll talk to my mother,' said Oliver. 'She promised to see to all the details.'

'That's very good of her,' Thomas said without surprise. Oliver's mother was a sensible, capable woman who was very good at organising and was only too happy to run everyone's lives for them. They went on discussing the wedding without consulting Leonie, who listened wryly and then went away to write to Dr Denis and give him a little vignette of the scene, hoping to make him laugh.

A few weeks after she returned, she got her first letter from Dr Denis and opened it with excitement over breakfast while Thomas Lincoln ate his toast and marmalade behind his *Times* and pretended not to be peering at her over the top of the paper.

Leonie ran her eye rapidly over the almost illegible lines of spiky handwriting which, French fashion, looked like the geometric dance of a spider who has fallen into an inkwell. She made out most of it and guessed the rest from the context, smiling as she heard about the people at the Mission. They were all well and busy, they all sent their love and Mtali was remembering to make the pork stew she had taught him so that Dr Denis no longer had curried pork or chicken at every meal.

Her stepfather lowered his paper, coughing. 'Any more tea in the pot?'

'Yes, of course,' she said, pouring him another cup.

'Thank you,' he said, stirring a spoonful of sugar into it

and eyeing her letter in a casual way. 'Interesting letter, was it?'

She offered it to him and he reacted as though he had been stung, jerking back in his chair.

'Good heavens, I don't want to read your post!' he exclaimed as if she had accused him of prying. 'I just asked to be polite.'

'Life seems to have gone back to normal in Mameea,' Leonie told him. 'The rebels are still hiding out in the mountain forests, but they aren't causing any more trouble in the rest of the country.'

'Oh, good, that's great news,' Thomas said, then snapped his *Times* open again and from the safety of its pages asked casually: 'He—er—your—er—father's well, is he?'

'He's fine,' Leonie said. 'Are you sure you wouldn't like to read his letter?'

'Quite sure,' she was informed, and her stepfather buried himself in the day's news after that. No doubt he was mildly curious about the man who had been her mother's first husband, it wouldn't be surprising, and, Leonie suspected, although her mother no longer lay between them as some bone of contention, there was in Thomas Lincoln's mind, at least, an element of continuing competition with Pierre Denis. He resented Leonie's renewed contact with her father, he was jealous and worried by it, but he had decided to pretend it didn't exist. It was the best way of handling the situation as he saw it—she was hundreds of miles away from her real father and in time, she imagined, her stepfather hoped she would forget all about the man living in the distant jungles of Mameea.

She was back at work now, of course, her days occupied with the routine of office duties, while at weekends and in the evenings she saw Oliver, but nowadays they were usually engaged on wedding plans of one kind or another. They didn't have time for the social life they had once had and all too often Oliver's parents were there, too, because both families were fully engaged with the wedding.

Leonie was only having one bridesmaid—her best friend from schooldays, Janice Green, a slim, quiet girl with a dark bell of hair and serious brown eyes, who worked in the personnel department of Thomas Lincoln's firm.

One lunchtime, over some cod and prawns in a bland cheese sauce, Janice asked abruptly: 'You do want to marry Oliver, don't you?' and Leonie looked up, startled.

'What?'

'Because if so, you aren't exactly giving a brilliant impression of the happy bride-to-be,' Janice observed, poking her prawns around with a disgusted expression. 'I should have had the shepherd's pie,' she added. 'This tastes like cotton wool in custard.'

Leonie looked at her own plate; she hadn't even noticed what she was eating, it was a long time since she had eaten anything, she noticed, her appetite was rather poor these days.

'I love Oliver,' Leonie said, and even in her own ears her words sounded oddly desperate, as though she was shouting to cover the fact that she wasn't sure about how she felt at all.

Janice didn't let it go at that, she looked up with a calm smile. 'You're very fond of Oliver,' she corrected. 'I know you are, you always have been, but do you love him? Do you really love him?'

Leonie prodded a prawn viciously and stuck it in her mouth, chewing it without enjoyment. 'How do I know?' she muttered in a mumble. 'I think so, I suppose so—

what do people mean by love, anyway? Look at all the married people you've ever met—I suppose they were in love, once, but when you're married you're just— married.'

Janice pushed her plate away. 'You poor idiot,' she said with friendly contempt. 'You're letting them push you into it, but you don't even know what it is you're being pushed into, do you?'

'Marriage,' Leonie said. 'That's what I'm being pushed into, and at least this time I got asked first, after a fashion.'

Janice stared at her, open-mouthed. Leonie stared back, wondering why Janice was looking like a boiled haddock.

'What's wrong now?' she asked impatiently. 'Why are you staring at me like that?'

'What do you mean—this time?' Janice asked care- fully.

Leonie flushed up to her hairline. 'What?' she fenced, and Janice kept her eyes on her boiled beetroot face.

'You said this time you got asked first,' Janice reminded her. 'What happened last time, and who did you marry?' She was laughing because she didn't really believe Leonie had been married before, she was teasing her, but she could see that there was something behind what Leonie had said if her friend was going to turn that interesting colour on realising she had given something away.

'Swear you'll never tell a living soul?' Leonie asked, tempted to tell somebody the secret of that crazy mock- wedding, and Janice, wide-eyed, nodded.

'Swear, cross my heart and hope to die,' she said rapidly, leaning forward across the table, and Leonie told her the whole story from beginning to end, this time filling in all the little holes she had left blank when she came back from Mameea.

Janice was fascinated, drinking in every word with eyes as big as saucers. 'Are you absolutely sure you aren't really married to him, though?' she interrupted suddenly, and Leonie laughed nervously.

'Help, I hope not! The man's a human steamroller,' she said, then looked at her watch and pretended to gasp. 'Look at the time, I must rush!' She was on her feet before Janice had time to say any more, fleeing with a flushed face. She wished she had never mentioned Greg to Janice, she had needed to talk about him, but now she would be afraid Janice would mention it next time they met, and Leonie was terrified of the feelings obsessing her. The more she tried to force them out of her mind, the more they seemed to dominate her thoughts, waking or sleeping.

How did you rid your memory of a man like Greg Thornton? She found herself drifting into daydreams about him all the time—remembering the mocking gleam of the grey eyes, the deeply tanned skin, the hard angle of cheek and jaw, the amusement and sensual promise of his firm mouth.

She had hoped that the passing of time would make his image fade, but she had been over-optimistic. She could not stop thinking about him. When Oliver kissed her lightly, he only reminded her of how she had felt when Greg's mouth burned against hers and his hands pulled her so close that she felt the imprint of his body from breast to thigh, the pressure making her heart race.

Awake or asleep, he never left her, and the ache of unsatisfied feeling drove her half crazy with frustration.

Even that evening, visiting Oliver's parents to discuss the wedding which was only two weeks away now, she kept thinking of Greg instead of listening to what was said. Oliver did most of the talking, but in the middle of an argument with his mother about the floral arrangements, he was called to the phone. He spoke into the receiver impatiently, then said: 'What?' in a voice which made everyone look at him in surprise.

He had gone red and was staring at Leonie, the look on his face making her suddenly very nervous indeed. He wasn't speaking, just listening to whoever was on the phone, but his lips were parted on a rough breathing which sounded like an effort to be calm.

'Yes, we'll be there in five minutes,' he said at last. 'No, I won't, not a word.' He put the phone down and Leonie waited, puzzled. 'We've got to go,' he said to his parents. 'Leonie, get your coat.'

She stood up. Something told her not to argue. Oliver looked as though he was waiting for her to argue and what would happen then would not be very pleasant, she felt, so she went and got her coat. She came back and the front door was open. Oliver's parents were standing there still looking worried and puzzled. Leonie thanked them for the meal and kissed them, then she joined Oliver in the car. She had no sooner closed the door than the car shot away at a terrific speed.

'What's wrong?' she asked in a faint voice, but Oliver didn't answer, he drove with his eyes fixed ahead and his jaw moving convulsively. She got the feeling he was getting ready to hit someone. She also got the feeling she had better be quiet and not ask any questions, so she sat back, with the patience of someone used to that sort of treatment from early childhood and waited for him to enlighten her.

He didn't, he did not utter a syllable until he braked hard outside her home and she got out. Oliver joined her and took hold of her arm in a tight, possessive clutch which made her look sideways at him.

'Just leave all the talking to us until we tell you to say anything,' he said, to her total astonishment.

'What are you talking about?' Leonie asked.

Oliver pushed her towards the house without replying. The front door was flung open and her stepfather stared at her, but he didn't say anything either. He stepped back and Leonie walked into the house. The sitting-room door was open and she automatically went into the room and then stopped dead, her face turning first white then a bright, scalding pink, as she saw the man sitting in a chair facing her, a glass of whisky in his hand.

Thomas Lincoln and Oliver took up positions facing her, between her and Greg Thornton, staring at her fixedly.

'Leonie,' said her stepfather in a terse voice, 'this man claims that you're his wife—is that true?'

CHAPTER SEVEN

LEONIE was too stunned to be able to say a word for a moment, her face confused and alarmed, while Greg watched her with sardonic mockery and her stepfather waited in increasing impatience for her to answer. When she didn't utter a syllable he burst out again: 'Leonie, what's the matter with you? Didn't you understand what I said? This fellow says he married you in Africa—it's a lie, obviously,' he added quickly almost as though daring her to deny that. 'I never heard anything so absurd in my life! Some sort of blackmail, of course, this is some trick to get money out of me, but if he thinks for a second I'll stand still for anything of the kind he can think again!'

The last words were hurled directly at Greg, who smiled lazily and without visible signs of alarm, before lifting his glass of whisky to his lips, his brown throat moving smoothly as he swallowed, his eyes observing Leonie over the rim of the glass while she stared back. She had told herself she would never think of him again, she would forget his very name, but he had been hovering in the wings of her mind ever since he put her on that plane to Cairo, and she couldn't take her eyes off him. The first time she saw him she had decided he wasn't particularly good-looking, but she had been mistaken; he was riveting, her eyes kept moving from the hard angle of his jaw to his amused mouth and then back up to meet the mocking grey eyes, and she could not clear her mind of the fog of feeling clouding it.

'Leonie!' Thomas Lincoln said loudly, and she jumped,

looking at him. 'Just answer the question,' he added. 'You aren't married, are you?'

'No, of course not,' she stammered, which made her stepfather and Oliver sag with relief, only then she went on to spoil it by adding: 'Well, not really—I don't know.' She gave Greg a pleading look. 'Are we?'

'What do you mean, are we?' Thomas roared.

Greg smiled. 'You might well ask,' he murmured. 'Coherent, isn't she? You'd better pray she never has to go into court and give evidence—a good counsel would make mincemeat of her in two minutes flat.'

Thomas Lincoln winced at the word court. 'Is that a threat?' he demanded, and when Greg laughed, looked at Oliver with open foreboding. 'I told you! Blackmail. I knew it the minute I set eyes on him!'

Oliver was staring at Leonie fixedly, his face dark red. 'Now look here, Leonie,' he began, taking a menacing step towards her, and Greg rose out of his chair, his glass slammed down on a nearby table. Oliver swung towards him and Thomas hurriedly moved between the two men.

'That won't solve anything,' he told Oliver, patting his arm.

'Wouldn't it, though?' Oliver asked wistfully. 'A good belt on the jaw might be the answer.'

For a second or two Thomas visibly hesitated, then he looked at Greg and measured the tall, powerful body with a faint sigh.

'Oh, sit down, Oliver,' he ordered, pushing him towards a chair.

Oliver had never argued with Thomas Lincoln in his life and he had no intention of starting now. He sank down, scowling at Greg, who stayed on his feet, poised there lightly, his hands on his lean hips and his well-cut dark jacket flung open.

Thomas Lincoln turned back to Leonie. 'Now, darling, don't get into a state about this—calm down, try to think clearly.'

Greg's mouth twitched, his lashes lowered against the tanned gleam of his skin which was even more striking when compared to the London pallor of the other two men. Leonie had never seen him in a suit before, it looked odd but it also looked very good on him, the dark material made him seem even taller.

'Tell us quietly what you mean,' her stepfather said in a slow, soothing voice. 'Now, were you ever married to this man?'

'This is crazy,' Oliver broke out. 'How can she be? Have you forgotten? She's marrying me! She can't be married already!'

'We know that, Oliver,' Thomas said irritably. 'Do be quiet while we try to get some sense out of her—she's obviously in a state of shock, look at her face.'

Oliver looked at it, without any sign of pleasure. 'I'm waiting to hear what the hell she meant by saying she didn't know if she was married to him or not. Either someone's married or they aren't—but they should damned well know which it is. I shall feel a real idiot if someone asks her if we're married and she babbles she doesn't know, she isn't sure.'

'You won't have that problem,' Greg informed him softly. 'I shouldn't let it bother you.'

Oliver half rose and Thomas Lincoln pushed him down again. 'Take no notice, he's trying to needle you.'

'He's succeeding,' muttered Oliver, even his ears red.

Leonie moistened her lips with the tip of her tongue. 'We did go through a wedding ceremony,' she said, and all three men looked at her, distracted from their eyeball to eyeball conflict.

Oliver said something very vulgar but Thomas Lincoln appeared to be entirely bereft of speech, opening and shutting his mouth like a stranded fish in a desert.

'But it wasn't real,' Leonie added quickly.

'Wasn't real?' Thomas Lincoln gasped, recovering his powers of speech at this glimmer of hope.

'I had to pretend to be his wife to get out of Mameea,' she said in a stammering flow of words, and explained what had happened. 'But we couldn't just forge a piece of paper, because the priest might have been shot if the government found out, so he pretended to marry us, but we weren't really.'

Thomas half-closed his eyes and groaned. 'Why ever didn't you tell us when you first got back? Why on earth did you hold back on us like that?'

'He told me I could forget about it,' Leonie said. 'And it wasn't a real wedding.'

'It was,' said Greg, and all three of them stared at him. 'Sorry,' he murmured, smiling. 'That's why I'm here. When Leonie's father got her letter and realised she was getting married so soon he asked me to fly over and explain—Father Armand really married us, it wasn't a sham wedding at all.'

'But you told me——' she began, and Greg interrupted.

'I know what I told you—I was wrong. I thought Father Armand had got my drift, it never occurred to me that he was going through a genuine wedding service. I'd meant him to do a quick patter, just to clear himself, but I should have known better. He assumed I'd realise he wouldn't fool around with a church sacrament. That's why he insisted you must have the marriage annulled when you got back to England.'

'Oh, no!' Leonie wailed, her face aghast. 'You mean that we——'

'We're married,' Greg said drily. 'Until we can get it annulled.'

Thomas Lincoln was very pale. 'Why the hell didn't you get here any sooner? She's marrying Oliver next week!'

'She's not, you know,' Greg pointed out. 'Unless you want to see her carted off to court on a bigamy charge.'

Leonie groped for the back of a chair and held on to it, staring at him.

'And I would have written if there had been time,' Greg went on. 'But I was kept pretty busy with the war until a few weeks back, I had no chance to drop in on the Mission, so I didn't realise that Father Armand had really married us.' He pulled a piece of paper out of his jacket pocket and handed it to Thomas, who looked at it in a dazed, disbelieving way. 'That's the certificate,' Greg told him. 'You'll need that for the court.'

Thomas held it, turning purple. 'What about the wedding?' he grated. 'What are we going to do about the wedding?'

'Cancel it, I'm afraid,' Greg said cheerfully, moving towards the door. 'I shall be in England for a few weeks,' he said, pausing there with a glance thrown back towards them. 'I'll be in touch in case you need further information.'

'How do we know this is legal?' Oliver demanded suddenly. 'It doesn't sound very legal to me, a hurried marriage in the African bush by some crazy priest.'

'It's legal,' Greg assured him. 'Father Armand registered it in the usual way—your lawyers can check it all out with the Mameea Government.'

'We'd better know where you're staying,' Thomas Lincoln muttered, and Greg pulled out a notebook, scribbled on it and handed the slip of paper to him.

'This is my sister's address, I'll be staying there this week, you can find me there if you need me.' He smiled at them in wry amusement. 'Look on the bright side, if you can—she could have been languishing in a Mameea jail if she hadn't married me.'

The thought did not seem to bring much comfort to either Oliver or Thomas; they stared at him blankly without replying, and Greg shrugged.

'I'll show myself out,' he offered and, since nobody bothered to reply, opened the door and went out.

'This is unbelievable,' Oliver muttered bitterly. 'I think I'm going out of my mind. How could she be so stupid?'

'Not even telling us what she'd done,' Thomas agreed.

'Not a bloody word,' Oliver fulminated.

'First thing tomorrow I'll get the lawyers on to it,' Thomas said. 'Heaven alone knows how long it will take them to sort it out, it could take months.'

'How could she do this to me?' Oliver groaned, not even listening. 'I shall look a complete fool! I suppose I'm lucky it didn't happen at the altar—can you imagine how it would look in the papers? Shock revelations at wedding, jilted bridegroom. My God, I'd be the laughing stock of the whole country!' He was apparently oblivious of Leonie's presence, not even looking at her. 'What if we'd actually got married? Then it would have been bigamy, that swine was right. She would have been arrested and I'd be hiding in some deep black hole hoping no one would find me.'

'On second thoughts, maybe I should ring MacAlpine tonight,' Thomas thought aloud. 'The sooner he's in on the picture, the better.'

'All my friends will laugh their heads off,' Oliver said

bitterly. 'I won't be able to show my face for months in any public places.'

'All the arrangements for the wedding will have to be cancelled,' Thomas Lincoln mused. 'That's going to cost a fortune, and all for nothing.'

Leonie swallowed and moved to attract their attention. 'I'm sorry, I'm really sorry,' she whispered, and both men stared at her coldly.

'So I should think!' Thomas snapped.

'Don't even speak to *me*,' Oliver told her with loathing. 'I won't want to set eyes on you for a long, long time.'

'The embarrassment!' her stepfather said.

'The humiliation,' said Oliver, writhing at the thought of it.

'Not to mention the expense,' added Thomas. 'Wedding cancellations, lawyers—they'll probably insist on flying to this godforsaken spot to check that this marriage is genuine.'

'I am sorry,' Leonie said desperately. 'I know I should have told you, but Greg did say it was just a charade and he told me I could forget about it.'

'And you believed him? Leonie, I ought to slap you,' Oliver said furiously, and for a second looked as though he might do just that, his eyes full of aggressive yearning. When they were small, Oliver had once or twice given her a slapping and Leonie remembered it all too vividly. She backed towards the door, nervously mumbling.

'I can't think why you agreed to the lunatic scheme in the first place,' Oliver ground out. 'It was sheer madness—marrying a perfect stranger!'

'I got bulldozed into it,' Leonie burst out, suddenly aggressive in her turn. 'Like you two, Greg Thornton doesn't give anybody a chance to think things over, he just rushes you into things and if you try to argue he makes nasty threats.'

'What sort of threats?' her stepfather pounced, narrow-eyed and excited at the word. 'That could be useful—what did he threaten to do to you?'

'Oh, shut up!' Leonie shouted, and ran out and slammed the door. She ran upstairs to her bedroom, vib-rating with a mixture of tears and rage, and heard the two of them begin their duet again, neither of them lis-tening to the other as they bewailed the situation.

She did not stop to put on the light, she halted in the middle of the room, brushing a hand over her wet eyes. They hadn't cared about her feelings, they had only cared about the embarrassment, the humiliation, the expense she was causing them, and it had hardly been her fault; she didn't want to be legally married to Greg Thornton, the very idea made her want to scream.

She bit her lip and walked slowly to the window to stare out at the night sky, watching the clouds scud before a blustering wind, a few pinpricks of light betraying the presence of a star or two.

Under her confused feelings of distress and anger ran another vein of feeling—Leonie did not examine it too closely, but she knew it was there and she felt slightly ashamed of it, because she was relieved. She was relieved that her marriage would not now take place as planned, she had been going crazy trying to think of a way of telling Oliver she did not want to marry him, and now fate had given her a breathing space. Fate—in the mad-dening shape of Greg Thornton, that was, and as her lips formed his name on a half sigh, half bitter mutter, she looked down and saw a car outside the house and inside it, his face dimly visible by the light of a nearby street lamp, sat Greg Thornton, smoking a cigarette.

Leonie didn't stop to think. She turned on her heel and went back down the stairs like greased lightning, not caring in that moment if her stepfather or Oliver heard her. She flung open the front door and charged down the path towards the gate, her blonde hair tossing about in the wind and a few drops of rain spattering her flushed face.

Greg's eyes slid sideways to watch her as she came towards the car, then, as she reached it, he leaned over and opened the passenger door on the far side and Leonie walked round to get in beside him. He had finished his cigarette and turned towards her, his elbow on the back of the seat, his head propped on his hand.

'How's the conference going?' he enquired.

'Couldn't you have sent me a cable or something? Couldn't you have warned me that the marriage wasn't just a sham? Did you have to walk in tonight out of the blue and tell my stepfather like that?'

He shrugged, quite unworried. 'They had to be told.'

'I could have broken it to them,' Leonie protested, paused and added: 'Gently.'

His mouth twisted in amused irony. 'I can imagine— what would you have done, told them a little of it day by day until they began to get some inkling what you were trying to say?'

'Well, I wouldn't have blurted it out the way you did,' Leonie said accusingly. 'You weren't exactly tactful.'

'Why hadn't you told them about it already?'

She went pink. 'I didn't see the point—after all, you had told me . . .'

'Yes,' he said, 'I know, I told you it was just a charade.'

'Well, you did! I thought it would just upset them, all for nothing, they would have started asking a lot of questions and it was pointless. I'd have found myself facing a long inquisition about you.' She broke off and he met her eyes shrewdly.

'They would have been curious about me?'

'Of course they would, what would you expect? If I'd gone through a marriage ceremony with you they'd have wanted to know everything about you, from the colour of your hair to what size socks you wear.'

Greg nodded, running a hand through his thick black hair while Leonie watched and wondered what it felt like, that vibrantly alive hair which sprang back from his brown face in an unruly mane. Her fingers curled on her knees, itching to touch it and find out, and she looked down to hide what she was thinking from him.

'You write a good letter,' Greg murmured, taking her by surprise, and she looked up again, her blue eyes wide and baffled.

'What?'

'You're a damned sight more articulate on paper than you are in conversation,' he added, and smiled at her, his face amused. 'I read your letters to your father.'

Leonie had a sensation of shock, of alarm, although she couldn't think why, she hadn't written anything to her father that she need be ashamed of or worried by, but she was disturbed to think of Greg reading the spontaneous, unconsidered words she had poured out on paper to her father ever since she got back from Africa. She had written to him openly and freely because she wanted so much to maintain the warm link she felt they had forged between them while she was at the Mission, but what she had written had been for his eyes only. She had not imagined anyone else reading them, and certainly not Greg Thornton. She couldn't even remember exactly what she had written, which worried her even more.

'My father showed them to you?' she asked breathlessly, and Greg's brows rose steeply.

'I certainly didn't burgle his desk to get them,' he drawled. 'Of course he showed them to me.'

'He shouldn't have,' Leonie muttered, very pink.

'Why not?'

'They were private.' She couldn't put it into words without betraying something she did not want to betray to him—that it made her feel naked to think of Greg reading her long, frank letters, it was like being caught in the bath by a windowcleaner, thinking yourself alone and suddenly finding yourself under observation.

'They were honest,' Greg said succinctly. 'And they made one fact painfully clear. You didn't want to go ahead with this marriage, you were desperately looking for a way out of it.'

Leonie's colour ebbed away and she caught back a shaken gasp. 'I never said that!'

'Not in so many words, no, but I read between the lines, and so did your father. We both saw the same thing.' He put out one hand and took her rounded chin, tilted it and looked into her wide, nervous eyes. 'It's true, isn't it? You don't want to marry this guy?'

'I don't have to answer that and I won't,' Leonie said crossly. 'It's nothing to do with you.'

'You don't love him,' he went on, unimpressed.

Leonie put her lips together and didn't say a word.

'And he doesn't love you,' Greg added, and her lashes fluttered but she didn't utter a syllable. 'I watched him and it was obvious. He's fond of you, but he isn't in love with you, by any means.'

Leonie knew that, he didn't need to tell her, but she didn't like hearing him say it and her face flowed with angry colour. 'Do you mind? Stop talking about my private affairs, they're none of your business!'

'Wrong,' Greg said calmly. 'I'm in this up to my neck,

in case you hadn't noticed. I hadn't meant to get so involved with you and I still can't quite work out how it happened, it was the last thing on my mind the day we met, but it happened step by step without my noticing how deep I was getting.' He ruffled his hair with an impatient, amused shrug. 'Women are like that—insidious. There's a pretty nasty disease you can pick up in Africa called bilharzia—a bug that lurks in the rivers. Anyone fool enough to swim in the water can pick it up, it burrows under your skin and you can't get rid of it.'

Leonie looked at him indignantly. 'You're so flattering, Mr Thornton, you leave me speechless!'

'Incoherent,' Greg corrected. 'As usual—never speechless, that I've noticed.' He smiled into her eyes and Leonie hurriedly looked away, a pulse beating at the side of her neck. The car seemed suddenly very small and very suffocating. She had never suffered from claustrophobia, but she seemed to be developing it now, there didn't seem to be enough air in this car, she was having trouble with her breathing.

'I watched your fiancé when I was in there,' Greg went on coolly. His breathing seemed perfectly normal, and Leonie resented that. Her presence wasn't having the effect on him that his had on her, but then she hadn't expected it would. He had probably known much prettier girls than her, he was much older than she was, and far more experienced and sophisticated, no doubt he had had a complicated love life, whereas Leonie had never had one of any kind, unless you counted Oliver, and she didn't. She had never met anyone remotely like Greg Thornton, and the sound of his deep voice beside her did drastic things to her pulse rate.

'The guy was livid,' Greg was saying. 'He was mad enough to punch my face in—but he wasn't jealous, he wasn't even thinking about you and me or wondering what you'd been up to with me . . .'

'I wasn't up to anything!' Leonie burst in hectically, very flushed. 'Oliver knows I wouldn't . . .'

'Oliver,' Greg said drily, 'never even thought about it. Oliver couldn't care less, it didn't enter his head. All he was thinking about was how he'd look when the news got out, what people would say and think. He didn't react like a man in love.' He took hold of her chin again, his fingers cool against her skin. 'And you don't react like a woman in love.'

Leonie was unable to answer, her shifting eyes confused and shy. Greg watched her, his glance hard and intent.

'You're not, are you? You're fond of him, he's fond of you, but that isn't a basis for marriage, and you'd begun to realise that, hadn't you? Your letters to your father practically spelt it out. You had him very worried, he didn't know what to do. He was thinking he ought to fly over and talk to you when I arrived.'

'Fly over here?' Leonie's eyes widened and met his, startled incredulity in them. 'My father was thinking of coming here?'

'He was wondering if he should, he didn't feel he could put it down on paper.' Greg grimaced. 'The trouble with feelings is that they're so intangible, and words do as much harm as good.'

'I wish he'd come,' said Leonie. 'I'd love to see him again—I miss him already, I hated having to leave the Mission. I'd hardly had a chance to get to know him, it would be wonderful to have him in England for a while.'

'I was coming to England, so I told him I'd deal with the situation,' Greg said calmly, and Leonie looked at him, taking a fierce sharp breath.

'You mean you stopped him coming? You talked him

out of it? Why, you really are ... who do you think you are? How dare you interfere like that?'

Greg stopped her angry stammering by the simple expedient of putting a hand over her mouth. Over the top of it she glared at him, her blue eyes shooting sparks of fury, and he regarded her with a wry smile.

'Your father is needed at the Mission—while he's away there's chaos there, but let's hope that situation won't continue. He's getting an assistant from Paris next month, a newly qualified doctor who was born in Mameea. The government is putting some money into the Mission hospital. Until now they've naturally concentrated all their available funds on the hospitals in the towns. Mameea is a very poor country and still undeveloped, but that's changing little by little. In a few years your father will probably have a well-equipped little hospital with a large medical staff. But for the moment, he can't afford to spend much time away from Mameea.'

He took his hand away and Leonie said in a low voice, 'Yes, I'm sorry, I wasn't thinking.' She looked away, tears pricking at the back of her eyes, and Greg watched her in silence for a moment. She couldn't have spoken to save her life, her throat ached with unshed tears and her voice would have betrayed the fact. She couldn't quite put it into words, anyway, the feeling sweeping over her. Inside the house behind them her stepfather and Oliver were no doubt still discussing the wrecked arrangements for the wedding, but they would not be thinking about her They never had, either of them. They never wondered how she felt or what she thought—she was like a pretty doll they both treasured and liked to have around, but she wasn't a person to them. She didn't matter, really matter. And she didn't matter to her real father, either. He cared about what she thought and felt, but his life had long ago been given to something else, to the Mission and to Africa. There just wasn't room in Dr Denis's life for her. She would always be on the periphery of his world, just as she was on the periphery of her stepfather's world and Oliver's world.

That wasn't enough for Leonie—she wanted to be the centre of someone's world, to belong, to matter. When she was at the Mission she had unknowingly been looking for her own place there, she had tried to make herself useful to them all so that they might let her stay, let her become part of their life. They had refused to allow it, though. All of them had taken the same attitude—they were warm and kind and caring, but they hadn't wanted her there. She hadn't belonged with them, they had more or less told her. Go back to where you belong, her father had said, Greg had said, Soeur Bernadette had said. But where was that? Not here—not with Oliver and Thomas Lincoln—she was certain of that now. She had had enough of being treated as some sort of mixture of doll and child. She was a woman; even if she had only just begun to realise all the implications of being a woman, and, it seemed to her, she was the only person in the world who was prepared to recognise the fact. Everyone else seemed to want her to stay the way she had been; a peaches and cream blonde with big blue eyes and nothing on her mind but new clothes and having a good time.

'This will give you a breathing space,' Greg said quietly. 'Don't let them rush you into a marriage you don't really want, neither of you really want. Face up to it. Be honest with yourself.'

'What makes you think I haven't?' she broke out angrily.

'If you had you would have put a stop to the whole idea long ago,' Greg pointed out.

'It isn't as simple as you think!'

'I realise it wasn't easy for you, but you wouldn't be happy with him.'

She moved restlessly and he sighed. 'Oh, you might have been content enough. He's obviously attached to you. He would take care of you, give you everything you wanted in the material sense, but there's a lot more to marriage than that.'

'You're an expert on the subject, are you?' Leonie asked in a barbed tone which surprised her as much as it surprised him.

He looked at her, his brows heavy. 'Don't snap at me, Leonie!'

'Don't patronise me, then,' she muttered.

'I'm just trying to talk some sense into you!'

'I'm quite capable of doing my own thinking!'

'So I notice,' Greg informed her with a biting emphasis. 'That's why you're about to marry a man you don't want.'

'I am very fond of Oliver!'

He laughed unpleasantly. 'Oh, you're *fond* of him, are you?'

Very flushed, she said coldly: 'Yes, I am.'

'But you don't want him,' Greg insisted, and the way he was looking at her made her move away slightly, her eyes sliding from his in an effort to evade the probe of his stare.

He waited and when she made no answer, demanded: 'Do you, Leonie?' His fingers fastened on her chin and turned her head towards him, her blue eyes hidden behind flickering lashes as she tried to pull her head away.

'Answer me,' he said huskily, running the tips of his fingers in brief, searing contact down the side of her cheek.

Her lashes lifted and their eyes met, a helpless, voiceless admission in her own. Her mouth was dry, her throat closed up in nervous excitement. Greg had moved closer, his eyes fixed on her face, and she was terrified of betraying the feeling inside her. She was aware of the pressure of emotions she couldn't control, she was afraid to admit. She wanted to touch his face the way he had just touched hers, let her fingertips explore the hard, cool structure of his face, feel the warm vibrant mouth moving against her lips. Her own feelings petrified her, but what scared her most was the thought that Greg should realise what was happening inside her.

'Do you even know what I'm talking about?' he asked, staring at her mouth, his eyes narrow and half-sheathed by lowered lids.

She swallowed, trying not to tremble visibly, because the way he was looking at her made her head swim, her body weak. 'I'd better go in . . .'

'Why?' he asked, moving closer, the looming dominance of his powerful body making her even more afraid. 'What are you so scared of?'

'I'm not!'

'No?' His mouth twisted ironically. 'What's this, then?' He placed one cool fingertip on the side of her neck where a pulse was beating violently, and at once other pulses began to pound in her body; at her wrists, at the base of her throat, a wave of heat rising inside her and making her eyes cloud so that she could hardly see him.

'Stop it,' she whispered in a low, pleading voice, but she didn't move because she couldn't, her body was rigid, waiting for him to touch her. She seemed to have been waiting for Greg to touch her for years, the nerve system of her body was going crazy as his fingers stroked down her throat. Her skin burned where ever he touched it, the brief tiny caresses had an intense sensuality which made her feel lightheaded.

Greg slowly bent forward, keeping her waiting, and she breathed painfully as she felt his lips against her throat. Her lids fell, she trembled, stifling a faint moan of pleasure as his mouth moved over her warm skin.

'Does he make you feel like this?' Greg muttered into her skin, one hand twining in her loose blonde hair, letting the curls trickle through his fingers. She felt his other hand on her waist, twisting her round to face him before the long fingers slid upward and touched her breast.

She gave a shocked intake of air, waking her out of the tranced excitement into which she had been plunged, and pushed him away with both hands, moving back against the door.

Greg sat up, surveying her with a lazy, satisfied smile which made her colour deepen. 'He doesn't, does he, Leonie? He does nothing for your pulse-rate at all. If you married him, you'd both be in trouble—I think you already realise that. You just haven't got the nerve to face it and do something to stop it happening before it's too late.'

'Your advice on marriage isn't worth having,' she stammered. 'If you're such an expert, why haven't you ever married? Or maybe that's why you haven't? You're the one who lacks courage, aren't you? I suppose no one you ever met was good enough for you.'

He frowned, his face hardening. 'It's different for me—my job would make it impossible for me to marry. I'm always on the move, I'm never anywhere long enough to settle down.'

Pain lanced through her and she turned to fumble with the door, desperate to escape before she said something she couldn't call back or deny later.

Greg moved abruptly, one arm moving round her to close over her hand on the door handle. She stiffened as she felt him right behind her, his thigh against her own, his face against her hair.

'You can't run away from it for ever,' he murmured softly. 'Sooner or later you have to face up to how you feel.'

Leonie ached with pain and misery. She wanted to be alone because she knew that even now she was on the point of beginning to cry, and she did not want to cry in front of him.

'As you're apparently against marriage in any shape or form, I can't see why I should listen to your advice,' she said.

'I'm not against marriage,' Greg denied. 'Happy marriages are fine.'

'Well, that's gracious of you,' she mumbled.

'My sister's very happily married,' Greg told her.

'Then maybe I'd listen to her,' said Leonie. 'Her advice might be worth having—yours isn't.'

'She'd tell you exactly what I'm telling you!'

'Will you open this door and let me out?' Leonie demanded.

She heard him breathing rapidly, impatience in the sound, then he released the door and she opened it and scrambled out of the car. She slammed the door behind her and ran away without looking back. She heard Oliver and her stepfather talking loudly in the sitting-room as she went back into the house. When she got back into her bedroom she walked shakily to the window, and saw Greg's car driving away, the red tail lights disappearing into the darkness while she watched.

The tears came painfully, crawling down her face and stinging as though they were hot. Her eyes ached with heat, too. She didn't draw the curtains, she stood at the window and let the tears force their way out of her in a silent gush, seeing the dark night sky through them as though it was raining. The wind scraped the branches of trees in the garden, bending them towards the walls of the house, and the billowing, streaming clouds flowed across the face of the moon as it rose above the houses far up on the hill nearby. All around her the quiet countryside of England breathed in the night, but Leonie was aware of being so alone she might have been up there on the pale, distant moon.

CHAPTER EIGHT

SHE slept badly that night and woke up to hear someone rapping on her door. Still half asleep, Leonie groaned: 'Mmm?' and the door opened and Thomas Lincoln stared across the room at her, his heavy grey head lowered aggressively and his brows contracted. For a few seconds Leonie didn't remember last night and was puzzled by the scowl he was giving her, then the memory rushed back and she flushed and bit her lip.

He came into the room and closed the door behind him. 'I want to talk to you,' he informed her in a voice she found distinctly threatening. She threw a hasty look at the alarm clock and was horrified to see the time.

'I shall be late for work,' she said, sitting up. Although she worked for him, her stepfather always insisted that she must behave like every other employee and get to work on time each day, more because of the feelings of other employees than out of any desire to teach Leonie punctuality.

Today, though, he brushed that aside. 'You aren't going to work,' he told her, sitting down on the side of her bed.

Leonie reached for the pretty apricot-coloured negligee which she had draped over the chair beside the bed last night and shouldered her way into it, frowning. 'Why not?' she asked.

'Oliver and I talked it all out last night,' Thomas said, and Leonie nodded.

'I know, I heard you.' They had been talking long after

she had got into bed, their voices rising and falling for another hour while she lay in the dark and tried to go to sleep.

'There's only one way of getting out of this without a lot of embarrassment,' her stepfather told her. 'You're going to have to go away.'

She stared at him, her lips parting on a faint gasp. 'Away?'

'Right away,' he insisted. 'And stay out of touch with your friends, don't tell anyone anything, don't write any letters or ring anybody up. You can go and stay with my cousin.'

'Cousin . . .' Leonie began, a horrible suspicion arising in her mind.

'Claudia,' he explained, and she groaned.

'Not Claudia, Daddy!' As a child, she had been sent several times to stay with Thomas Lincoln's cousin, Claudia, who lived and worked on a small sheep farm in Cumberland, and it was laughable to describe a visit to her as a holiday. She rose at dawn and expected guests to do the same, and she expected guests to help with all the work around the farm. Leonie had always crawled back to Surrey after a visit to Cousin Claudia, needing a holiday to get over the experience.

'Don't argue, Leonie,' her stepfather said irritably. 'Claudia's the ideal person to have you, she never asks questions.'

'She never listens, either,' Leonie said gloomily. In the long dull evenings on the farm, Claudia read books on sheep diseases and filled in her piles of government forms of which she had an unending supply, they seemed to come by every post, but she never talked.

'If you want something kept quiet, Claudia's place is the perfect spot,' Thomas went on. 'She never sees anyone but her sheep, nobody will know you're there.'

'Not even Claudia, probably,' Leonie said drily, wondering why she was being put into isolation like someone with a contagious disease.

'While you're up there, Oliver and I will tell everyone that you're ill,' her stepfather said, ignoring her, and it all became very clear. Who had thought of it first? she wondered. It was a brilliant idea, whoever it had been. It would work, she could see that. Oliver wouldn't be a figure of fun after all, he wouldn't have to hide from his friends or feel a fool. 'Poor old Oliver,' everyone would say sympathetically, and pat him on the shoulder, rather than smile behind their hands and say: 'Poor old Oliver,' in a very different tone.

'What have I got?' she asked out of a sense of curiosity, and her stepfather looked at her blankly.

'What?'

'What have I been struck down with—measles or pneumonia?' Leonie asked lightly. She had been right first time—they were treating her like someone with a contagious disease.

'Leonie, don't be frivolous about this,' Thomas Lincoln warned her impatiently. 'This is no laughing matter. We thought we could say you'd picked up some bug in Africa which had only just hatched out and the doctors weren't sure what it was so you were being kept in observation.'

Leonie was awed. 'Brilliant,' she said. 'That's really clever, did you think of that?'

'Well, yes, actually,' her stepfather said, looking slightly self-satisfied, not to say smug. 'We can be vague, then, make it very unspecific and once this ridiculous business has been sorted out you can come back home and marry Oliver as planned.'

Leonie didn't answer that remark. 'When do I leave?' she asked, and her stepfather glanced at his watch.

'No point in ringing Claudia during the day, she never answers her phone. It will have to wait until this evening. I'll ring her, make sure she'll have you there and then Oliver will drive you up there tomorrow morning. Today, you'd better stay in the house, keep out of sight. Tell Mrs Wood you feel ill, that would be a good idea. You can have a few symptoms—headache, sore throat, that sort of thing.' He got up and walked to the door. 'I must get to work. Now, Leonie, not a word to anyone and that includes Janice. Not a soul, is that understood?'

'Yes,' she said meekly. 'Daddy,' she added and he paused, looking back. 'I am sorry I've caused all this trouble,' she said.

He looked at her gloomily. 'I know, you can't help it, I suppose,' he said, and went out, closing the door firmly.

Leonie heard his car drive away a few moments later and then she slid out of the bed and went to the window. Drawing the curtains, she inspected the new day with a sense of more optimism than she had gazed at the sky the night before. A few hours' sleep made quite a bit of difference to how you saw things. Maybe a long visit to Cumberland would be rather fun, and it would certainly give them all a chance to take a new look at the situation. Maybe Oliver would start using his brains for more than working out new sales campaigns and fresh approaches to accountancy.

Mrs Wood came in every day to do the housework but, since none of them were ever there to keep an eye on her, she had a very individual sense of time and arrived when she felt like it, which this morning proved to be more towards eleven than nine, the hour she was supposed to start work. Leonie was downstairs writing a long letter to her father in Mameea, and Mrs Wood looked at her in surprise and a faintly defensive wariness.

'Hallo, Leonie, thought you'd be at work. I'm running a bit late this morning, my husband took sick . . .'

'So did I,' said Leonie, putting a hand to her head. 'In fact, I should have rung you, Mrs Wood—I don't know what's wrong with me, but it might be contagious, so you'd better not come near me.'

Mrs Wood withdrew to the door again, her thin sharp face alarmed. 'Whatever is it, dear?'

'Maybe something I picked up in Africa,' Leonie suggested, and Mrs Wood was out of the door now, hovering at the threshold.

'Have you seen a doctor? Want me to ring him?' She peered at Leonie, her brown eyes inspecting her closely, and Leonie tried to look wan and frail, sighing.

'I'm seeing him later, he's coming round here.'

'Ah, doesn't want you at the health centre, in case,' Mrs Wood observed knowingly. 'That's sensible, never know what you can pick up in places like that, all sorts of nasty diseases going around.' She was a short, spry woman in her late fifties whose chief interest in life was gambling; she played Bingo every weekend, did the football pools and bet on horses. She had disapproved of Leonie's trip to Africa, which she now proceeded to point out at length. 'I told you before you went, didn't I say? Go to a place like that you could go down with anything. Not to mention other things, you never know what will happen in places like that. Safer to stay at home.'

'Yes,' Leonie said when she was allowed to say anything. 'You can do the other rooms, then, Mrs Wood, but you'd better not come in here. I wouldn't want you to catch anything.'

'Righto,' said Mrs Wood, and Leonie added that Mrs Wood might as well get off home early if Mr Wood was ill, too.

'He may need you,' she said, and Mrs Wood thanked her and went out to do a rapid job on the house. She was gone two hours later, leaving Leonie a salad in the kitchen.

'Of course, I won't tell anyone,' she assured Leonie as she left. 'I won't tell a living soul. You won't want it getting out—start a panic, that could.'

Leonie smiled as she heard the front door close. Mrs Wood would no doubt be on her way to tell everyone she knew that Leonie had been struck down by a mystery disease, undoubtedly contracted in Africa.

Leonie finished her letter to her father, which was the longest she had ever written him, and added the postscript: please, please, don't ever let anyone read this. She sat by the window, reading the scribbled pages through, hesitating. Should she send it? It was far more frank than anything she had ever written before, and reading it made her feel stupid. It had helped to write it all down, her own feelings of confused and puzzled uneasiness, her sense of having changed, grown up, without anyone around her seeming to notice. Dr Denis was the only person who might understand, but now that she saw it all written down in black and white she knew she couldn't send it. It was far too personal, far too revealing. She sighed and gathered the sheets together, was about to rip them across and consign them to the wastepaper basket when she heard a car stop outside, a door slam.

She looked out of the window and saw Greg striding up the path, the wind blowing his black hair into a whipped confusion.

Leonie felt herself tighten inside. She dropped the letter on the desk and ran to the door. Greg rang the bell sharply, and Leonie put on the door chain and opened the door a fraction.

'What do you want?'

He surveyed her through the crack, his expression wry. 'Don't be ridiculous, Leonie, open the door.'

'I don't want to talk to you—go away!'

The grey eyes held hers, forced her to look back, refused to let her drag her gaze away. 'Open this door, Leonie,' he said softly, his voice veined with menace.

Leonie opened the door, furious with herself, and he came through it with a contained violence which warned that he was in no mood to put up with any displays of independence from her. The minute he was in the house she felt that odd claustrophobia taking her over again, she was conscious of a tightness in her chest, a heat inside her veins, a sense of weakness which made her want to sit down before she fell down.

Greg pushed her back into the sitting-room, where she sank into a chair to hide from him the fact that her body was trembling. Her hands twisted in her lap, she looked at him defiantly. 'What are you doing here?'

'I rang your father's firm and asked to speak to you and was told you were at home, sick.' He gave her a sardonic smile. 'Original of you.'

'It wasn't my idea, it was theirs,' she said with her usual coherence when he was around.

'I wondered if it was,' he said. 'Been on to their lawyers, have they?'

'I don't know, they don't tell me anything—I expect so.' She looked away and added: 'They've thought of a plan—I'm to go away and they're going to tell everyone I've caught some bug in Africa and the wedding has to be postponed until I'm better.'

'Clever,' he said. 'I wondered what they'd come up with—and afterwards? When they've sorted out our phoney marriage, what then?' He was watching her closely and she couldn't meet his eyes because his presence made her so nervous.

'I don't know,' she said, and got up impulsively, trying to smile. 'Would you like some coffee? I was just going to make some.' She was on her way to the door before he had time to answer. She felt him move, but he didn't follow her and she flew into the kitchen and took the coffee out of the wall unit, catching sight of her own face reflected in the glass door. She stood there staring at herself at last admitting the truth, a wave of self-knowledge sweeping over her as she looked at her over-bright eyes, her flushed skin, her trembling mouth.

She was in love with Greg. She had been from the minute she set eyes on him on that dusty air strip in the jungle, and it had made radical changes in her. It had not been the impact of Africa, or getting to know her real father, which had accelerated the slow process of her struggle towards maturity—it had been meeting Greg Thornton and falling in love with him. He had added a new chemical to the confused mix of her feelings.

Automatically she spooned coffee into the percolator and switched it on, took out coffee mugs and arranged them on a tray, found the sugar bowl and cream jug and set them out. Her palms were slippery with perspiration and she felt faintly sick. She leaned on the wall, her eyes closed, listening to the percolator bubbling, the clock ticking, but above them all she heard the fast, fierce rhythm of her own heart.

When she took the coffee into the sitting-room, Greg stood up and took the tray, placed it down on the low, highly polished coffee table while Leonie sank into a chair nearby.

'Black or white?' she asked politely, thinking how useful social courtesies were, they made it possible to have a conversation with someone when what you wanted to say could not be said.

'Black, please,' he said, and watched her pour the coffee, his gaze on her bent head making her hand tremble. 'That pot's too heavy for you,' he said, seeing the traitorous little tremor, and Leonie smiled, somehow.

'Sugar?'

'Please,' he said. 'One lump will do.'

Leonie ceremoniously deposited one lump of sugar in his cup and handed it to him before she poured her own coffee.

'Are you on leave in England?' she asked as she nursed her cup.

He nodded. 'I haven't been back here for two years, I spent my last leave in the Middle East. There've been a lot of changes since I was in England last.'

'Yes, haven't there?' Leonie said blankly, scouring her mind for something else to say. She opened her mouth to say something neutral and safe and instead found herself asking: 'Why are you here?'

Greg put down his coffee cup. 'Why am I here now?' he queried, and she nodded. He smiled teasingly at her. 'Last night I chucked a bomb in here—I wondered what sort of fall-out there'd been.'

He had come because he was curious, nothing more. Leonie drank her coffee, it was bitter but she made herself drink it.

'Where are they sending you?' Greg asked.

'Cumberland.'

His brows lifted steeply. 'Cumberland? That's a hell of a long way away.'

'My stepfather has a cousin there who'll let me stay for a while. Oliver's going to drive me there early tomorrow morning.' Her tone had a dull, flat sound and Greg did not miss that, his eyes shrewd.

'How are they treating you this morning? Are they still angry with you?'

'Oh, I'm in the doghouse,' Leonie shrugged. 'I can't blame them, I should have told them what happened in Mameea.'

'Why didn't you, Leonie?' She looked at him, opening her mouth, and he held up one hand: 'I know you say it was because you thought the whole thing had been a pretence—but even so, I'd have thought you would have mentioned it. After all, you had to run for your life, it was a pretty hair-rising experience, it seems odd you didn't mention it to them.'

'They would have asked a million questions,' Leonie muttered.

'And you didn't want to answer any questions about me?' Greg probed, and she looked down, playing with her cup, fingering the handle and tracing the pattern on the smooth glaze.

She did not answer, and after a pause, Greg said: 'What's this place in Cumberland like? Are you going to enjoy being there?'

'It's a small hill farm,' Leonie told him. 'You can see for miles up there—you get a wonderful view of sheep.'

Only after she had finished speaking did she realise how bitter her voice had been, how low and harsh, and she sat there, horrified, hearing the echo of her words all around them.

'You don't want to go,' said Greg, and she didn't answer. 'Why don't you tell them so? Stand up to them, tell them to go to hell.'

Leonie shrugged hopelessly, and Greg stood up, making her jump. Her eyes flew to his face, but he was already walking out of the room, without a word, and Leonie was stricken. He was going, she might never see him again.

He was always walking away from her and each time it hurt more. She waited to hear him open the front door but instead heard him going upstairs. Surprised, she stood up, beginning to collect the coffee cups, then she heard Greg moving about in her own room, overhead. She froze on the spot, listening in disbelief to his footsteps, the sound of the wardrobe opening, the rattle of coathangers.

She put down the tray and ran out of the room, taking the steps two at a time and bursting into the bedroom, to halt in amazement as Greg flung a pile of lingerie on the bed.

'What are you doing?' she demanded, and without looking at her, Greg said crisply: 'Packing.'

'What are you talking about?' She was baffled and alarmed as she watched him neatly folding some of her clothes into a small suitcase which he must have found in the back of the wardrobe. Leonie leapt across the room and pushed his hands away. 'What on earth do you think you're doing?'

Taking hold of her wrists, he held her arms down at her side, eyeing her with amusement. 'Isn't it obvious? I'm packing for you and then I'm going to drive you to stay with my sister.'

Leonie was completely taken aback. 'Your sister?'

'She'll be glad to have you to stay for a while, and she doesn't live at the back of beyond. You won't have to hold conversations with sheep, although you may have to look after her two offspring at times. Marcia tends to dump them on the nearest person whenever she wants to take off for town. She's pretty ruthless, so watch her, don't let her turn you into a dogsbody.'

'What are you talking about?' Leonie burst out. 'I can't go and stay with your sister, I don't even know her!'

'She's very hospitable. She enjoys having guests. Her husband is a workoholic who's rarely at home, which may explain why their marriage works so well. He doesn't have to put up with Marcia all the time, he has an escape route.'

Distracted by this information, Leonie said bitterly: 'Why are you so cynical?'

His brows lifted derisively. 'Is that how I sound?'

'Yes, that's how you sound. I don't suppose your sister would be too pleased to hear the way you talk about her.'

'Marcia has heard me talking about her all her life— she's a couple of years younger than me and from the day she was born I've been complaining about her.'

'That must make you very popular with her!'

'We get on very well, as it happens,' he said with a slightly defensive grimace.

'It doesn't sound like it.'

'Don't form judgments until you have some idea what you're talking about,' Greg warned.

Leonie tugged at her imprisoned wrists. 'Will you let me go? You're shutting off the blood to my hands and I'm getting cramp.'

He released her hands but seized her shoulders instead, the strong fingers firm and compelling. 'Now, listen to me, Leonie . . .'

'Why should I listen to you? How dare you come bursting into my life, pushing me around as if I were a child?' She was so angry she was shaking, her face very flushed. 'I've had enough of being treated like that by everyone around me! Nobody will let me make my own decisions, nobody will leave me alone.'

'If I left you to your own devices, you'd go trotting off to this sheep farm to spend weeks with nothing to do but admire the view. Is that what you want?' His grey eyes held her blue ones forcibly, his face hard. 'Is it, Leonie?'

'That's beside the point. I can't just go off with you like this, my stepfather and Oliver would be demented!'

'Leave them a note, tell them where you are. If they want to discuss it, they can come over and talk to you any time they like.'

'They'd be on the doorstep ten minutes after reading my note,' Leonie said with grim certainty. 'And then they'd make me leave and I'd feel a fool.'

'They'd make you leave?' Greg repeated, eyeing her contemptuously. 'And you talk about making your own decisions?'

Her face held shifting uneasiness. 'I'm fond of them!' she defended. 'They'd go spare if I went off with you! They'd wonder what I was up to.' She could have bitten off her tongue as she heard herself saying that last sentence, wishing she could recall it, especially when she saw the smile which flashed into his grey eyes.

'What would they think you were up to?' he enquired lazily, his black head at a mocking slant.

Leonie stayed silent, looking away, but knowing that he was watching her. He knew perfectly well what she meant, the implications lay between them almost visibly.

'Don't they trust you, Leonie?' he asked in a soft, teasing voice, and her colour rose higher.

'They don't trust you,' she snapped, and Greg laughed, then his face changed and he said in a cooler tone: 'You don't want to go to Cumberland, it was obvious from the way you talked about it. Why let them dictate what you do?'

'I can't just descend on your sister—how would you explain what I was doing there?'

'I've often mentioned your father to her. Why shouldn't I bring his daughter to stay for a week or two?'

'She's bound to think . . .'

'That she's meeting her future sister-in-law?' he mocked.

'I'm sure you'll make it clear that I'm nothing of the

kind,' Leonie muttered, and Greg laughed again.

'Then she'd decide that your role in my life was a very different one,' he said, watching her.

'You and your sister obviously think alike,' she muttered, and heard him start to laugh.

'You should watch what you say,' he teased and, reflecting on what she had said, Leonie inwardly writhed with embarrassment. 'Is that what you suspect?' he enquired. 'Do you think I have you marked down as a possible conquest?'

'Well, if you have, forget it,' snapped Leonie, so furious she was barely ably to speak at all. 'Is that why you keep urging me not to get married?' she added with hardly a pause, her hands clenched at her sides. 'Because, if so, even if I wasn't married I wouldn't . . .'

Greg waited as she broke off the stammered flow of words and bent towards her, asking softly: 'Wouldn't what, Leonie?'

She didn't answer, couldn't force a syllable out, stunned into silence and deeply aware of the way he was looking at her, his eyes fixed on the tremulous, vulnerable pink curve of her lips. She was both afraid of the possibility that he might kiss her and aching for him to do it, and, torn between the two, she jerked her head away, presenting him with the taut line of her cheek.

After a long moment Greg said in a dry voice: 'I wish you weren't so young, you're playing way out of your league. You haven't an idea what this is all about, have you?'

'You keep saying that!' She had found her voice, but it didn't sound like hers any more, it had a husky, adult sound, thickened by emotion and roughened by anger. 'Maybe I would understand if you didn't keep talking in riddles.'

'If what I'm talking about is a riddle to you, maybe it's just as well that I don't make myself any clearer,' he murmured, releasing her. She watched him, working out what he had meant, while he turned to close and lock the case.

'Come on, get your coat,' he said, turning back to her. 'We'll leave a note for your stepfather and get going.'

Leonie hesitated, still unsure what to do—should she go? Greg watched her face, sighing.

'Don't worry, Marcia will make a more than adequate chaperone. If it will ease your mind, let me assure you that I have no deep, dark motives for taking you there. I just think it might be more pleasant for you to stay with a lively family than to go trudging off to the wilds of Cumberland to gaze at sheep.' He eyed her mockingly. 'At least it will give you an idea how a happy marriage looks.'

'Are you sure she won't mind having me landed on her?'

'Quite sure—would you like me to ring her first to make quite certain?'

She hesitated again, then nodded. 'It would mean I was expected,' she said, and Greg picked up the case and walked out of the room. Leonie followed and watched him pick up the phone and start to dial. She wrote a note to her stepfather while he talked to his sister, trying hard not to listen.

'Marcia, Greg here. Would it be okay for me to bring someone to stay with you for a few days?' He paused and listened, his face amused. 'A girl,' he said, and was obviously interrupted again. 'She's Dr Denis's daughter and she's twenty,' he went on after a long pause.

Leonie pushed her note into an envelope and wrote her stepfather's name on it, stood it on the mantelpiece where he would see it as soon as he arrived. She heard Greg laughing and then he said: 'We'll be with you in around two hours. Okay?'

He put the phone down and Leonie looked at him questioningly. 'She says you're very welcome,' Greg informed her. What had his sister said that made him laugh like that? she wondered, but she did not ask. She had a feeling that either he wouldn't tell her or she wouldn't like the answer.

They left the house and got into his car after Greg had stowed her case in his boot. Leonie sat anxiously in the passenger seat as they drove away, feeling very unsure of herself.

The day was crisp and bright and clear, one of those days in autumn when the sun is high in a still blue sky and sounds seem to carry enormous distances across the English fields. The leaves hung on the trees lightly, some already floating off and drifting into piles in the hedge-rows. Everything she saw seemed new-washed and changed, she felt she saw through eyes which had never seen before, everything had a clarity and beauty she had never noticed.

She looked sideways at Greg, seeing him with that strange new insight—the strongly moulded features, the tanned skin and hardbitten grey eyes, the firm, passionate mouth and determined jawline. Greg carried his nature in his face, he was a million light years ahead of her in the maturity stakes and she couldn't imagine she would ever catch up, but she felt, oddly, that today she had taken a giant stride in that direction, although she had no idea how or when.

CHAPTER NINE

ON the long drive to his sister's house, Leonie imagined what would happen when her stepfather found her note, grimacing to herself. He would be furious, of course. This was the second time she had acted in defiance of his wishes and this time she had not even discussed it with him. If she had, if she had waited for him to come home before making up her mind whether or not to accept Greg's invitation, she knew Thomas would have put every possible obstacle in her path. He would have been aghast at the very idea that she should go and stay with Greg's sister. It didn't bother her stepfather that if she went up to Cumberland to stay with his cousin Claudia for weeks, she would be bored out of her mind. All he was thinking of was his own interests. He and Oliver wanted her safely out of sight while they told their version of why the wedding had been postponed. Why should she let them go on for ever manipulating her as if she were a puppet?

'What are you brooding about?' Greg asked, shooting a glance at her sideways.

'Nothing,' she said, starting.

'Sulking?' he asked. 'If I pushed you into this, it was because I could see you weren't going to argue with your stepfather and it's time you did. You keep telling me you're an adult, but you won't act like one.'

'I'm here, aren't I?' Leonie retorted. 'You didn't have to carry me out of the house. I made up my own mind.'

'With a little help from me,' Greg drawled, one brow arched in derisive comment.

Leonie stared at the landscape flashing past, the dark branches showing more and more through their tattered remnants of leaves, the fields still and empty under that blue autumn sky, with, here and there, the smoke from burning stubble winding upwards in the distance giving the air that characteristic scent of vanishing summer.

'It isn't easy,' she said confusedly.

Greg was silent for a moment, then said in a gentler voice: 'It never is, Leonie, nobody promises you an easy ride into being an adult. Being responsible for yourself is a tough business.'

'They *do* love me.'

'Of course they do, but that has nothing to do with it. They have to learn to love you and let you go.' He gave her a quick smile, his tanned skin crinkling around those grey eyes. 'And you have to learn to love them and leave them.'

'Is that your recipe for a good life?' she asked with a lingering echo of bitterness, and he frowned.

'What's that supposed to mean?'

'You told me you don't believe in marriage—so I imagine that loving and leaving is what you do believe in,' Leonie muttered, bending her head, her blonde hair blowing around her face and obscuring it from him.

He didn't answer, and she gave him a sidelong, searching look. He seemed unaware of her gaze, his face set in a heavy frown, his mouth a hard line above that determined chin. Inside her, her heart moved painfully as she looked at him. How many times had she woken up in the night, since she got back from Africa, remembering him like that?

'You fire a string of personal questions at me,' she said. 'You give me endless advice on how to manage my life. But you never answer me when I ask you a question.'

'Maybe I don't know the answer,' Greg said in a clipped voice. 'If you'd asked me that a couple of years ago, I'd probably have agreed without needing to stop and think. I've always believed that the only way to do my job is to travel light, and that means never leaving anything of yourself behind, walking away from any relationship, knowing that you're as free as the wind.'

Leonie listened to his quick, curt voice, her mind intent on what he meant as much as what he actually said.

'And now?' she asked huskily. 'Can't you say that now?' Hope made her so tense it hurt, her skin was ice-cold.

He was silent for a moment, then he shrugged. 'I haven't changed my mind about the best way of doing my job, no. I lead a nomadic life, I'm always ready to fly off at a moment's notice, my case is always packed. One day it's on the cards that I might not come back alive. Is that any life to offer a woman?'

Although the final question was mostly rhetorical, she sensed that he paused to wait for an answer, and turned towards him, her face pale. Greg looked round at her, feeling the movement, and their eyes met and held, his stare probing her eyes in a frowning interrogation.

'I suppose it would depend on the woman,' Leonie said, and she nodded briefly.

'Would you put up with living like that?' He didn't give her any chance to reply, he laughed and turned away. 'Of course you wouldn't. And even if you tried, it wouldn't work out. I've seen it happen over and over again—colleagues of mine marry and try to go on working in the field, but sooner or later they give up and take their wives home because it eats a woman up to live on the edge of danger all the time. They can't take it, and their men can't do their job properly if they're always aware that their marriage is at risk.'

'But . . .' she began, and Greg interrupted harshly.

'Let's change the subject. I'll tell you something about Marcia, shall I? Her husband is a civil engineer—he's based in London and works for a firm that specialises in building roads and power stations overseas. Ted spends a lot of time abroad. They have two kids—Mandy who's six and Edward who's eight.'

Leonie listened with one part of her mind, but the other part was absorbing what he had said about himself, understanding the things he had not said. She had no idea how he felt about *her*, but now she had some glimmering of understanding about how he felt about marriage. It would interfere with his job and, to Greg, his job came first.

His sister lived in a small village in Suffolk within sight and sound of the sea, the air heavy with salt and the crash of the waves on jagged rocks keeping up an unceasing tumult as they drove through the village street in the late afternoon. Small white timber-framed houses and whitewashed flint cottages gave the place a quaint, old-fashioned air, the street winding narrowly between them.

'It's lovely!' Leonie exclaimed, sitting up to stare around her in delight. 'I love those old cottages.'

'They look as if they're falling down,' Greg said drily. 'One good wind and the whole place could blow away.'

'Don't be so unromantic!' she said crossly. 'I think it's beautiful and I love it.'

'But then you're a romantic and I'm not,' Greg told her, and she sensed that the remark covered far more than just her delight in the peaceful little village. 'I often wonder how Marcia can stand it, living here day in, day out,' he added. 'The night life is nil and in the winter it's so quiet even in the daytime that you can almost hear a pin drop.'

'Maybe she likes life quiet,' Leonie suggested, and he laughed.

'You haven't met Marcia yet, I should keep the guess-work until you have.'

He turned up a high-banked lane at the end of the village and a moment later turned into a broken-down old gate to pull up in front of a rambling white house of indeterminate age. Leonie looked at it curiously and decided it was two cottages knocked into one at some stage of its history.

The front door flew open and out tumbled a confused mass of arms and legs which sorted itself out into a tall, slender woman with brown hair and a smooth, tanned skin; a skinny little boy in well-washed jeans and a blue sweater; a little girl dressed identically but with a yellow sweater, and two dogs which were making most of the noise, barking and panting excitedly as they converged on the car. Greg had climbed out, which was a mistake as he was at once engulfed by the advancing dogs and children. Leonie slowly got out and the woman smiled at her over the car bonnet.

'Hallo, I'm Marcia Lucas—sorry about the racket, they aren't trying to eat Greg, only making sure he knows how glad they are to see him.'

'You could have fooled me,' said Greg, pushing the dogs down as they licked his face. 'Stop it, you noisy hounds! Marcia, call them off. Look at my pants—covered in dog hair!'

'It'll brush off,' Marcia said cheerfully. She had an oval face within which her features fought each other—her nose snub and comical, her eyes warm brown, her mouth firm and determined. Across the bridge of her nose was sprinkled a good crop of freckles and in her white sweater and blue jeans she looked more like a boy than a woman in her thirties; her body flat and lithe. Leonie searched her face for some resemblance to Greg and found none. The two children, however, were very like their mother—in colouring and build and feature.

Marcia grabbed them, a hand on the shoulder of each, and swivelled them towards Leonie. 'This is Mandy,' she said, and the little girl gave Leonie a gap-toothed smile, one of her front teeth conspicuous by its absence. 'And this is Edward.' He grinned, tossing back a flopping lock of rich brown hair from his temples.

'I'm Leonie,' she said. 'Leonie Lincoln.'

The children giggled, and their mother sighed. 'They have a weird and wonderful sense of humour,' she half apologised. 'Any little thing amuses them.' She released the children and turned towards the house. 'Come in out of the cold. We get the wind from the sea here, it blows right across the fields at us.'

Leonie glanced towards the sea, which made a grey line on the horizon, framed between twisted, wind-beaten trees whose gnarled branches were already half bare, their leaves ripped away by autumn gales and rustling in dry, brown tides along the hedgerows. The fields running to the sea were pastures grazed by sheep, their white forms visible in the descending dusk as they moved across the tussocky grass; low green hedges marking out the fields, the barbed wire brambles heavy with glistening black-berries in places.

'You live in a beautiful place.'

Greg laughed shortly. 'Leonie fell for the village the minute we drove into it,' he told his sister.

Marcia eyed him with sisterly impatience. 'Of course she did, it's a wonderful village, the prettiest in Suf-folk.' Looking at Leonie, she added: 'Still unspoiled, thank God, most of the houses are very old and we want to keep it that way.'

'It was dead and alive when we were young and it hasn't changed,' said Greg, and Leonie looked at him quickly.

'You lived here when you were young?'

'We were both born here,' Marcia told her.

'You didn't tell me that,' Leonie said to Greg, and he shrugged.

'Didn't I?' He knew he hadn't, he hadn't even mentioned it, and that must be deliberate. She wondered why he hadn't told her, the omission seemed puzzling. She looked at the low white house and asked Marcia: 'Did you live here, then?'

'Yes, although it was two houses then, of course. We lived in this part.' Marcia gestured to the left half of the building. 'My husband bought up the second cottage after we were married and we converted the two into one to give us more room. They're eighteenth century, the rooms were very small.'

The dogs and children had surged back into the house and the adults followed them. Greg had walked round to the back of his car and opened the boot to remove Leonie's case, which he carried into the house, walking behind his sister and Leonie, listening as Marcia chatted.

'I've given you a room with a view of the sea, I thought you would like that. None of the bedrooms are very big, I'm afraid, and the ceilings are rather low, be careful not to bang your head on the door. We don't want you to start off your visit by knocking yourself out. My husband is always forgetting to bend down. He's over six foot and constantly walks into things when he's here.'

'It's very nice of you to let me stay,' Leonie stammered shyly, and Marcia gave her a cheerful smile.

'Not at all, I like having visitors.'

'Who wouldn't, living here?' said Greg.

'I notice you always come to stay when you're in England,' Marcia told him. 'If you didn't love it, you wouldn't come.' She grinned at Leonie, her brown eyes teasing. 'Take no notice of him—he gives Wildhay a bad press, but he loves it secretly.'

Leonie glanced at Greg, who was looking amused. 'That's an unusual name, Wildhay,' she said to Marcia, who became very lively, nodding, her face enthusiastic.

'Centuries ago it was called Wildhaven, and when you see the sort of storms we get in the autumn and spring you can understand why it got the name—but Suffolk people believe in saving time and trouble, so they abbreviated it to Wildhay over the years.'

'Shall I take Leonie's case up to her room?' Greg asked, and his sister nodded.

'I've put her into the end room.' She looked at Leonie, her face enquiring. 'Would you like to go up and unpack and have a wash? Have you driven far? If you're very tired . . .'

'We've only driven from just outside London,' said Greg. 'I'll take her up.'

'Would you like some tea?' Marcia asked Leonie, who gratefully said that she would indeed.

'I'll make it while Greg's showing you upstairs.' The dogs and children had vanished into a sitting-room from which Leonie could hear the sounds of a television. The house was divided by a narrow passage from which two doors opened and at the end of which lay a flight of stairs. While Marcia vanished into the room opposite the one into which the children had dived, Greg led Leonie towards the stairs. Their wooden treads were worn hollow in the middle with generations of feet and they creaked like the timbers of a tilting ship as Leonie followed

Greg up to the bedrooms.

'Ted took out the other staircase,' explained Greg. 'It gave him more room for the dining-room and kitchen. He believes in open plan living and large rooms, but they left the bedrooms more or less as they found them, except that he modernised the bathrooms and put central heating into the rooms upstairs.'

'It must be useful to have a husband who's in the building business.'

'Ted's job has nothing to do with building houses,' said Greg, walking down the corridor to the end of the house. He opened a door and let Leonie walk into the bedroom in front of him. She stood there, looking around, while Greg put down the case. As Marcia had said, the ceiling was low and the walls solid, the floor sloping dramatically so that you felt you walked on a ship's deck as you crossed the room. The floorboards were bare, stained a dark brown, with brightly coloured mats strewn here and there. The bed was modern, the rest of the furniture matching it, the warm rosewood glowing softly as Greg switched on the blue silk bedside lamp.

Leonie walked over to the window and looked towards the distant sea which was being swallowed into a drifting haze of smoky shadows as night fell.

'This was my room,' Greg said abruptly at her back.

She looked round, surprised. 'When you were a child?' He nodded.

'I hope I haven't turned you out of it,' she said, watching him, and he shook his head.

'No, I'm using a room on the other side of the house. I always sleep there when I'm staying with Marcia and Ted.' He threw a look around the room, his eyes shadowed. 'I don't like this room.'

'Why not?' Leonie asked quietly.

He turned and leaned towards the window, one hand propping him up, resting on the wall, his body very close to hers, his face hard. 'When I was a boy I used to stand her night after night, looking out at the sea, listening to it, longing to get away from here.'

'Because it was too quiet?'

He hesitated, a visible uncertainty in his face. 'Does it matter why?' His hand dropped and he turned. Leonie moved at the same instant, intending to step back out of his way, and her foot skidded on the polished floorboards, sending her sliding off balance. Laughing, Greg caught her and held her. Her eyes lifted to his face, a confused awareness in them, her body trembling as she felt his hands on her waist.

'Leonie,' Greg muttered, his voice deep and husky, his eyes fixed on the passionate curve of her mouth, and her trembling increased, her breathing rough and unsteady. 'Don't look at me like that,' he said, the words blurred by the rapidity with which he said them.

'Like what?' she asked, yearning to feel his mouth touching hers and hardly aware what she was saying because the ache of hungry passion had become a driving necessity. She was scarcely conscious of herself at all at that moment, only conscious of the need rising inside her.

'I wish you weren't so damned young,' Greg said almost inaudibly, then he bent his head and she moved towards him to meet his kiss, her arms going rounds his neck. His lips tasted cool from the wild rush of the sea air, then the coolness went and he began to kiss her with heated abandon, locking her against him with both arms around her, holding her so close she was conscious of every inch of the taut, male body pressing against her. Weak with desire, her ears pounding, Leonie yielded to him. An urgency began to build between them, the kisses demanding her total response, and with eyes closed, Leonie let herself slip into the cloudy regions of passion through which he was leading her, and to which she was totally new.

Greg pushed her backwards and she sank down on the bed, her lids flickering, her hands running in quick, restless little caresses from his nape to his shoulders and down the long line of his back. When she felt his fingers against her breast a faint moan broke from her and Greg lifted his head to look down at her. His hand moved away and without opening her eyes Leonie caught it and held it, silently pleading with him, lifting her head to search for his mouth again.

'Leonie,' Greg muttered thickly, then he wrenched himself away and stood up. She felt cold and rejected. Her eyes opened and met his fixed, frowning stare, and she felt tears pricking behind her lids.

'You're just a baby,' Greg told her. 'Do you know what you're doing? I shouldn't have kissed you.' He moved restlessly, sighing again. 'I want you badly, but ...' Breaking off, he moved at a rapid stride to the door. 'Come down when you're ready,' he said, and was gone, the door closing with a crash behind him.

With the stiff, careful movements of someone afraid of pain, Leonie sat up stiffly, then sank down on the bed again. She stared at the floor, her face pale, pain and humiliation deep inside her. She didn't understand Greg and he had no intention of explaining himself — whenever he came close to revealing what went on inside his head, he hurriedly closed the door on her again.

After a while she got up, unpacked, hung her clothes in the wardrobe and tidied them neatly into drawers, then went to the bathroom. She took ten minutes to wash, change her clothes and renew her make-up.

When she went back downstairs in a pair of white jeans and a blue sweater, she found Marcia and her two children in a room which served as a combination of kitchen and dining-room. It was long, low-ceilinged and had rough-plastered white walls on which hung a bewildering number of pictures, prints and childish drawings which seemed to have no rhyme or reason, had merely been hung there higgledy-piggledy, the sheer mass of colour somehow becoming harmonious.

'Hi, I was just wondering if I should send up a rescue operation in case you'd got locked in the bathroom and couldn't get out,' Marcia said, giving her a grin.

'Edward did,' said Mandy. 'He got locked in and Mummy had to climb up a ladder and get through the window.'

Edward went pink and punched her, grimacing silently.

'The lock sticks,' said Marcia, separating her children absentmindedly with one hand while she put a plate of home-made biscuits in the centre of the table with the other.

'Uncle Greg went for a walk,' Mandy said, and Leonie met Marcia's eyes, looked away at the sharp intelligence in them.

'He took the dogs, but he wouldn't take us,' Edward said resentfully, scowling.

'You talk—the dogs don't,' their mother pointed out. She smiled at Leonie. 'Do sit down and have your tea.'

'We made the biscuits,' said Mandy, pushing the plate at Leonie with a coaxing smile which displayed her missing tooth to perfection. She had her mother's snub nose and freckles and that gamin smile had charm.

Leonie gingerly accepted a biscuit cut in the shape of a rabbit and bit it. The children watched eagerly. It was a shortcake mixture which had been overbaked until it was the colour of Mandy's brown eyes, but it was very edible.

'Delicious!' smiled Leonie, and got a broad grin from each of them. Edward gallantly offered her the plate again and she took one biscuit, refusing to have any more at their entreaties. 'I'm slimming,' she said, and they beamed again.

'All right, you can eat some now,' their mother said wryly, and the small hands grabbed. Leonie watched the biscuits departing in rapid succession and stifled a giggle.

'They love their own cooking,' Marcia told her, offering her a cup of tea. 'They much prefer it to mine. When you've made something yourself it tastes much better.'

'Can we go and watch TV now?' Edward asked, his eye on the kitchen clock which hung on the wall behind them.

'For half an hour, no longer,' said Marcia. The children flew to the door and to their departing backs she warned: 'Bath-time in exactly three quarters of an hour!' The door slammed behind them and she sat down with a long sigh. 'By the time they're in bed every night I feel around a hundred! I don't know where they get their energy—I wish I had some of it. You have to be permanently on your toes to stop them turning the house into a disaster area.'

Leonie laughed. 'They're gorgeous, I'm sure you wouldn't be without them.'

'No,' Marcia agreed, picking up her cup and sipping the tea with closed eyes. 'Oh, peace! I love them most of all at night when they're asleep.' She put down her cup and glanced at Leonie. 'Greg has told me so much about your father, I almost feel I know him, but he didn't ever tell me Dr Denis had a daughter.'

'He didn't know,' Leonie said, and explained the background to her childhood while Marcia listened, watching her.

'And you flew all that way to meet him?' she asked, her face curious.

'Wouldn't you have wanted to know what he was like?'

'I suppose I would, but it's surprising that you weren't rather bitter about him. I think in your place, I would have been.'

'I was, too, at first, but once I'd met him my whole attitude changed.' Leonie's face shone, her blue eyes warm. 'He's a marvellous person.'

'So Greg tells me,' Marcia murmured. 'But then Greg would admire him, they have a lot in common.'

'Have they?' Leonie looked at her searchingly and Marcia met her eyes with a thoughtful expression.

'Tell me if I'm prying but exactly what is going on between you and Greg? I'm happy to have you here, but I can't remember Greg ever bringing a girl home before and I can't help being curious.'

'It's a long story,' Leonie explained, unwilling to tell the whole of it. 'To be frank, I'm not sure myself what's going on between Greg and me. I don't think he's sure, either.'

Marcia laughed. 'You don't surprise me. For a clever man, my brother is a little slow on the uptake at times. When I told him I was marrying Ted, he tried to talk me out of it for the craziest reasons.'

That didn't surprise Leonie, but she asked: 'What *were* his reasons, or would you rather not talk about it?'

'Greg knew that Ted wasn't the type to stay in one place for long and he was afraid I'd be unhappy. I told him to mind his own business. I knew what I was doing, Ted and I had been frank about it. Ted is often away for months, working on remote sites where a woman is out of place. When we first married, I went with him, but once the children started to arrive I stayed at home. It was all a question of compromise. Once I'd made up my mind it was Ted I wanted, I just had to accept him the way he was, which meant he was going to be away a lot. I don't like it. I'd rather have him with me all the time. But given the choice between Ted or no Ted, I knew I'd put up with all the problems. And when the kids are old enough, I plan to go with Ted whenever I can. It's worked out, even Greg has to admit that.' She grinned at Leonie. 'Reluctantly, of course. Greg hates to admit he could have been wrong.'

'I don't think he's reluctant to admit it,' Leonie said. 'He told me you had a very happy marriage.'

Marcia looked pleased. 'Did he? That's nice. It's true, too. We do, but because we work at it. We know the problems and we try to find a way round them. We write to each other, talk on the phone as often as we can, and Ted makes sure he spends as much time at home as he can.' She got up and began to clear the table. Leonie helped, carrying china to the kitchen sink and offering to wash up.

While they worked, Marcia said: 'Greg was influenced by our parents, you see. Their marriage didn't work out. My father was very much like Greg, he had a hankering all his life to go to sea, but my mother cried whenever he talked about it. They led a cat-and-dog life for as long as I can remember, and I think Greg was afraid that if I married Ted the same thing would happen with me.'

'Oh, I see,' Leonie, light dawning suddenly, murmured, and Marcia threw her a quick look. 'That explains why he keeps telling me how important it is to marry the right person,' Leonie explained.

Marcia looked fascinated. 'Does he? How interesting.'

Leonie felt herself blushing. 'No, you misunderstand,

he doesn't mean . . .' She broke off and Marcia laughed.

'Doesn't he?'

Leonie turned away and fidgeted with the tea towel she was holding. Knowing the background of Greg's childhood made his attitude to marriage and women far clearer. Growing up in a house with quarrelling parents must have made him very wary of marriage while at the same time making him yearn to travel. Greg had imbibed his father's dreams of a wandering life at such an early age, he might not even realise how deeply influenced he had been by hearing his father talk about travelling and sailing to strange, distant lands. She remembered his face as he told her how he had stood at the window in his bedroom at night watching the sea and longing to get away—to escape from the antagonism between his parents, no doubt, to find the dream his father never stopped yearning for, the dream which he had unknowingly inherited but made his own.

'I suppose we're always influenced by the way we grew up,' she said half to herself.

'Of course,' Marcia agreed. 'I expect that's why I picked Ted in the first place. I loved hearing him talk about his work, the countries he went to—I could listen for hours. I suppose I expected a man to love travelling, having heard my father talk about it so much. But I'd learnt from my mother, too, and I realised I had to stay out of Ted's way, not try to make him give up what he loved. Loving someone doesn't mean you have the right to blackmail them into doing what you want them to do.'

Was that what Greg expected from her? Leonie wondered. Did he suspect that if he let her any closer she would try to blackmail him into giving up his job?

The door opened and Marcia looked round, amusement in her face as she met Greg's narrowed eyes. 'Hallo, we were just talking about you,' she confessed cheerfully.

He came into the room, his eyes shooting at Leonie. 'Oh, were you?' he enquired with faint menace.

Marcia said drily: 'Take no notice of the scowl, Leonie—his bark is worse than his bite.'

'I've no intention of taking any notice of either,' Leonie said with bravado, and Greg eyed her consideringly.

'Trying to talk like a grown-up?' he mocked.

A beam of yellow light cut across the drawn curtains and they all heard the sound of a car engine cutting out. Marcia gave a surprised exclamation. 'Now, who on earth can that be at this hour? I'm not expecting any visitors. Isn't it amazing—some days I never see a soul, then in one day I get a perfect stream of visitors.'

Leonie had a flash of intuition, her eyes meeting Greg's, and he frowned, moving to the door.

'I'll go,' he said, and his sister looked surprised.

'It isn't for you, is it? Are you expecting anyone?'

Greg didn't answer, but vanished. Marcia looked at Leonie, her face curious. 'Do you know what's going on?'

They heard Greg open the door just as someone began pounding on it with what Leonie suspected to be clenched fists, then Thomas Lincoln roared like an unfed lion.

'Where is she? How dare you? I've a good mind to get the police on to your track! This is kidnapping, you know.'

Marcia looked at Leonie, a question in her eyes, but Leonie was too intent on listening to the raised voices to take any notice of her.

'You're not getting away with this,' Oliver's voice grated. 'Don't think for a minute you are!'

'You'd better come in,' said Greg in a controlled voice. The door slammed and then Greg appeared in the doorway of the kitchen, and over his grimly set shoulders

Leonie saw her stepfather and Oliver, their faces flushed with temper, their hair blown into disorder by the sea wind.

Greg looked across the room at her, but spoke to her stepfather as he stood to one side to let the other two men enter the room. 'Don't try to bully Leonie or you'll have me to deal with!'

Leonie's eyes widened and brightened. Thomas Lincoln gave Greg a surly look but Oliver advanced towards her in a threatening way without taking any notice of Greg.

'What do you mean by bolting with that guy? Haven't you made enough trouble for us?'

'Don't shout at me,' said Leonie, with one eye on Greg's frown, trying to look as helpless as possible. 'I won't be bullied.'

Oliver gave her an enraged glare. 'Bullied? I haven't even started yet! You've forced me to drive all this way straight from work and I'm in no mood to put up with your childish tantrums!'

She moved to run towards Greg and Oliver grabbed her arm. A second later Greg had knocked him away with a force that sent him staggering. Recovering his balance, Oliver leapt back towards them with the eagerness of a hungry tiger released from a cage, his face filled with aggressive enthusiasm.

'What do you think you're doing?' Marcia demanded, stepping into his path and bringing him to a reluctant, panting halt.

Since he made no effort to enlighten her, Marcia looked at her brother, raising her brows. 'Well, Greg? This is my house, haven't I a right to know what on earth is going on in it?'

Greg shrugged. 'If they'd given me time, I'd have introduced them.' He waved a hand towards Thomas. 'This is my sister Marcia. Marcia, this is Leonie's stepfather, Thomas Lincoln.'

Thomas gritted his teeth and forced a mimicry of a smile. 'How do you do?'

Leonie turned away in case she began to laugh. She heard Marcia say politely: 'How do you do?'

Oliver growled: 'And I'm Leonie's fiancé, but your brother didn't bother to tell you that.'

Leonie felt Marcia staring at her in open surprise, but she kept her eyes lowered.

'You're not,' Greg said coolly. 'How can you be engaged to Leonie when she's married to me?'

Leonie lifted her head and saw Marcia sink, open-mouthed, into the nearest chair, looking from one to the other of them with deep interest.

'What are you up to?' Thomas Lincoln demanded, scowling. 'You abduct her from my house . . .'

'How can I abduct my own wife?' Greg asked sweetly.

'Not for long, she isn't,' Oliver muttered furiously. 'It doesn't mean anything, you told us so yourself. As soon as we've had it annulled . . .'

'We've changed our minds,' Greg informed him, and a silence fell on the room.

Leonie was staring at Greg who looked back at her, his mouth twisted in a wry little smile. What had he meant?

That question was uppermost in Thomas Lincoln's mind, too. He, however, decided to ask it in a voice which rose like thunder, 'What the hell does that mean?'

'We're married and we're staying married,' Greg said calmly. 'Leonie isn't going to be shunted off to Cumberland, she's staying here with me and we're staying married.'

Leonie sat down in the chair next to Marcia, avoiding her eyes, and ostentatiously folding her hands in her lap.

This was one time when she was happily going to allow a man to make up her mind for her, she decided.

Her stepfather was glaring at her. 'Leonie, what have you got to say?'

Leonie gave him a placatory little smile. 'Nothing.'

'I'm speaking for Leonie, too,' Greg said with arrogant self-confidence, and she demurely lowered her eyes.

'Leonie!' Thomas grated. 'Have you lost your senses?'

Probably, she thought, but didn't say a word, and after regarding her with frustrated rage for another moment, her stepfather turned back to Greg.

'You don't expect me to take this seriously?'

'Oh, but I do,' said Greg. 'We've made up our minds, and you'd better take it seriously.'

Leonie was so happy she wanted to sing, but she just sat there and listened. Greg had made up his mind and she took it very seriously indeed.

CHAPTER TEN

She made no effort to enter into the noisy, angry discussion which followed, although both her stepfather and Oliver attempted to get her to speak. Whenever they threw a phrase her way, demanding that she make her own position clear, she merely looked at Greg and he spoke for her. All her life men had been doing her talking for her and she had resented it, but tonight she was quite content with the way things were going—indeed, for the first time she felt it was herself who was manipulating events, using silence as a weapon. She wanted Greg and she no longer cared what she did to get him.

At last Oliver and Thomas departed, even angrier than when they had arrived.

Her stepfather turned at the door and looked at her across the room. 'When you've come to your senses you know where we are,' he told her. 'For the moment, I fully intend to find out how legal this marriage is, because I don't trust this man an inch. He's taking advantage of you, in my opinion, but I don't blame you, Leonie. You're too young to know what you're doing. If you come home, you needn't be afraid you'll have to face recriminations.' There was a trace of a plea in that and Leonie looked at him with wry affection.

'Don't be too angry, Daddy,' she said. She loved him and she wanted him to accept that she wasn't going to marry Oliver, but she did not want a final breach between them. That would hurt them all.

Her stepfather didn't answer, he just tightened his lips

and went after Oliver. She heard the front door bang behind them. Marcia got up and walked to the door, too.

'I'd better give the children their bath,' she said, tact-fully removing herself without so much as a hint of a question, but then, no doubt, during the argument which had raged between her brother and Thomas Lincoln she had picked up a great deal of information about what had happened between Leonie and Greg.

Greg walked to the window and stood there, staring at the windy darkness. Over his shoulder Leonie could see the branches of trees moving and between them, caught like a white balloon, the moon shedding a pale radiance over the night sky.

'In a couple of years I'll be forty,' he reminded her. 'You'll only be twenty-two. I've been living alone since I was eighteen, and living alone is a habit which isn't easy to break.'

She waited without attempting to argue, sensing that all the argument had been done in his own head. She only had one trump card and she wasn't going to play it until she was sure it was the right moment.

'I don't know if I could live with anyone,' he went on. 'I'm not used to having anyone to consider but myself. I'm probably pretty selfish.'

She smiled to herself. 'No probably about it,' she said. 'You *are* pretty selfish.'

'I'm no bargain for a girl of twenty,' Greg said in a flat, tired voice, his body held in that stiff tension. 'But I could get a job in England, give up my foreign posting.'

'Why should you?'

He turned then, looking at her quickly. 'I can't ask you to share the sort of life I lead.'

She looked interested. 'Is it exciting? What do you get up to in Cairo? Wine, women and song?'

'Don't be ridiculous,' he said, but he laughed. 'You know what I mean—I'm always on the move around Africa, I have to be ready to fly off at a moment's notice and I never know how long I'll be away. I'd sometimes have to leave you in Cairo for weeks on end.'

'I've always wanted to travel,' Leonie said. 'I loved Africa—if you had to go away I'd probably go and visit my father at the Mission. It would give me a chance to get to know him better.'

'It's dangerous,' said Greg, almost pleading with her. 'No sanitation to speak of, insects and snakes—anything could happen to you.'

'I could get run over by a bus in London any day of the week,' Leonie pointed out. 'That doesn't stop me going up to town to shop.'

He moved restlessly, looking at her with deep feeling in his face, his eyes uncertain. 'You may think now that you'd be prepared to put up with it, but you'd be miles away from everything you know.'

'Except you,' said Leonie, getting up. She walked over to him while he watched her intently. Now was the time to play her only card, she sensed. She put her arms round his neck and looked at him, her blue eyes full of unhidden passion. 'I love you and I want to be with you.'

She felt him resist for a moment, both physically and mentally, his body as taut as wire, then he put his arms around her and kissed her hungrily, holding her as though he was afraid to let her go, so tightly she could only just breathe.

'I love you,' he muttered as his lips lifted from hers a moment later, and he framed her face between his hands, looking at her with tenderness. 'You're so young, I've no right to do this, but I've got to have you. I need you.'

Leonie smiled, running a possessive hand down his

cheek, delighting in the feel of his skin under her palm, the strength of that bone structure as she traced it from his cheekbones to his jaw. 'I need *you*,' she said huskily, watching the flare of passion in his face.

Greg was silent for a moment, staring at her. 'It won't be easy,' he warned.

'You told me nothing ever was,' she reminded him. 'Like the Girl Guides, I'm prepared.'

He laughed shortly. 'I must be crazy even to consider it—I know all the problems, you don't. What if you get tired of living abroad and want to come home in a year or so?'

'Can't we let time take care of that? You can be sure that even if I did, I wouldn't try to blackmail you into throwing up your job. I'd do what Marcia has done, work out some way of living with it.'

Greg's lashes flickered and Leonie surveyed him with sudden dry, amused and loving comprehension. 'Is that why you brought me here? So that I could see how your sister coped with the problems of a man who refuses to stay for long in one place?'

He didn't answer, his lips crooked in a smile of self-deriding admission, and Leonie surveyed him with an answering smile, her face amused.

'How devious!'

'I wasn't being devious so much as trying to find out if it could work out for us. I wanted you here where I could see you and I knew that if you went off to Cumberland I wouldn't see you again.'

She looked at him searchingly. 'Yet you let me fly back go England, you didn't intend to see me again then.'

Greg sighed. 'I told myself I'd be insane if I let you get under my skin. I'd convinced myself that getting married was not for me. I hadn't expected to meet anyone I couldn't live without.'

Leonie liked that, her eyes widened and glowed, and he smiled at her wryly.

'I guess I knew the minute I saw you on that air-strip—I looked at you and thought: that's for me, but you were so young. I kept telling myself it was madness even to look twice at you.' Bending his head, he kissed her neck lingeringly. 'You're beautiful, that's the trouble. I want you too badly to be able to let you go again.'

She moved closer, putting her head down on his chest, hearing his heart beating under her ear. 'I like your sister very much, but couldn't we have our honeymoon some-where more private?' she whispered. 'Somewhere where we can be alone?'

She felt Greg's heartbeats racing faster, then he took hold of her shoulders and moved her away, looking down at her with a wry face. 'There's just one problem there,' he said. 'We're not married.'

Totally at sea, Leonie regarded him questioningly. 'What are you talking about?'

'I lied,' Greg confessed. 'We're not married—what I told you in the airport at Mameea was the truth. The certificate is just a bit of paper. Father Armand perfectly understood what I wanted him to do—he just read us the marriage ceremony, he didn't actually marry us.'

'He didn't?' she repeated, her heart sinking.

'Your father and I cooked the idea up between us. We both wanted to stop you marrying Oliver, but there wasn't time to try to talk you into taking a stand against the idea. I had to make sure the wedding didn't happen, so I came along and chucked a spanner into the works.'

Leonie's brows furrowed as she understood him. 'I see.'

'It would have given you a breathing space,' Greg said quickly. 'Given you time to know what you wanted. Your father was worried, he could tell you didn't want to marry Oliver, your letters made it as clear as crystal.'

'How shall I tell my stepfather?' Leonie thought aloud, wincing. Once Thomas knew she wasn't really married to Greg, he would make every effort to come between them and Leonie wouldn't have the protection of that little bit of paper which, legally, made her Greg's wife, and took her out of her stepfather's protection.

Greg considered her with uncertainly. 'I suggest we tell him after the wedding,' he said, and she looked at him quickly. 'If we tell him now there'll be one almighty row, and I've only got a month's leave. If we get married right away it would solve all the problems. If we have to wait until your stepfather is prepared to approve of our marriage, we might have to wait for a long time.

'We'd definitely have to wait for a long time,' Leonie said with a wry grimace. 'Once he knows I'm not really married to you at all, he'd try to talk me into going through with marrying Oliver. It's his life's dream, he won't give up on it without a fight.' She sighed. 'Neither will Oliver. You're right about how he feels, but although he isn't in love with me, he's obstinate and he hates to have his plans upset.'

'He's going to have to grin and bear it, then,' said Greg with aggression. 'But before we make a definite decision, Leonie, I want you to be quite sure you know what you're doing. If we're getting married, I want it to last.'

'So do I,' she said seriously. 'It will, Greg. I'm certain, I don't need time to think about it. But are you sure?' She put a hand to his face gently, looking at him with intent eyes. 'You have more doubts than I do—I only had one, whether you loved me.'

'I do,' he said huskily. 'And I'm sure.' He smiled, putting both arms round her again. 'Once I'd started to try to figure out how I could make a marriage between us work, I knew I was going to marry you if I possibly could. You can always give yourself good reasons for doing what you want to do in the first place—however many reasons you come up with for doing something you don't want to do, you find it very hard to go through with it. Haven't you ever noticed that?'

'Frequently,' she said, laughing.

'One person who won't be surprised is your father,' Greg said suddenly. 'I told him how I felt when I was at the Mission before I flew home. That's why he showed me your letters, he thought I might be in a better position to help you than he was—he felt that if he tried to interfere, Thomas Lincoln might turn very nasty.'

'I'm sure he would have done,' Leonie agreed. 'He doesn't like my father much.'

'Of course he doesn't,' Greg said drily. 'He did your father a great wrong and we always hate people we've injured. We feel guilty and so we need to turn our feelings of guilt into something we can manage more easily.'

Leonie sighed. 'It seems a pity, I love them both, I hate to think of them resenting each other. What did my father say to you? When you told him how you felt?'

Greg smiled and she looked sideways at him teasingly. 'Aren't you going to tell me?' she asked.

'You really want to know?'

'Of course I do, I'm dying to know.'

'He told me to go and get you if I wanted you, that life was too short to miss any opportunities of being happy and I was a fool to hesitate about taking the chance.'

Leonie began to laugh, her eyes tender and delighted. 'Oh, he's such a wonderful man! Isn't he marvellous?'

'I won't argue with that,' Greg said, bending his head to look at her with a smile. 'But I wonder what you would have said if he hadn't agreed with you?'

'I'd have said he was wrong,' Leonie told him firmly. 'But he does agree with me. He once told me that loving was all that mattered, everything else followed on from that. Without it, life was meaningless and ugly. With it, there was always hope.' She sighed deeply. 'His letters kept me on the right track since I got home. I could easily have let Oliver and Daddy swamp me, smother my mind again, but my father's letters kept blowing on the flame, making me certain what I ought to do.'

'Your father's a born subversive,' said Greg. 'I see what he's been up to—keeping your little local rebellion brewing with his propaganda about love. I wonder what was in his mind?' He looked at her probingly. 'Your letters didn't mention me very often and only casually when my name did crop up.'

Her eyes teased him. 'I'm not completely stupid, writing too much about you would have been a dead giveaway.'

'I wonder if he read more between the lines than I imagined,' Greg mused.

'I shouldn't be surprised.'

He surveyed her with a wry smile. 'I hope you're not seeing me as a father figure—it wouldn't be surprising if you did, given the gap in our ages, but I don't see you as some sort of proxy daughter, Leonie. It wouldn't work between us that way.'

'I'm up to my ears in father figures,' she told him. 'I don't need any more, I have enough trouble with the ones I have already.'

'Thank God for that,' he said. 'I sometimes wondered.' There was a brief pause and he asked: 'How do you see me?'

'Don't you know?' she asked, looking intently at his hard, strong mouth, putting a finger on it to trace the line of it.

'I wasn't sure,' Greg admitted, kissing her fingertip. 'I took a chance that you wouldn't contradict me when I told your stepfather we were staying married. I thought I knew how you felt, but I wasn't sure.'

'What you mean is, you just went ahead and arranged my life for me,' Leonie teased, but with contentment in her blue eyes. 'As dictatorial as ever, in fact.' She had no intention of telling Greg that from the minute she saw him she had known he was the fantasy she had always had locked inside her head, the special man, the midnight lover who came in dreams and was gone by morning. She had never expected to meet a man who matched that blueprint, but when she did, she could not get him out of her mind. She had known it was no longer a fantasy. In real life love means that the midnight lover stays till morning.

There was a faint question in Greg's eyes as he watched her. 'You *are* sure, aren't you, darling? I know I took it for granted that you felt the way I did, but ...' He paused, smiling wryly. 'You're not used to hiding how you feel.' His eyes warmed with passionate amusement as she blushed and laughed.

'You're fond of your stepfather, aren't you?' he asked, his face anxious. 'I hope it isn't going to upset you too much to quarrel with him over me.'

'Oh, he'll huff and puff for a while,' Leonie told him calmly, 'but he'll get over it. He has Oliver, you see. Oliver means more to him than I do. He always has. Oliver's going to run the firm one day, but my stepfather thought he would get the best of both worlds if I married Oliver. That would have satisfied his conscience about me. He could leave the firm to Oliver without a qualm then. He'll do that, now, anyway.'

'You won't mind missing out on a fortune?' Greg asked, looking at her hard.

She laughed. 'I couldn't care less. I was never interested in the firm—Oliver's welcome to it.'

Greg relaxed. 'And when will you marry me? It will have to be a quick, civil wedding, so that we can fit in a honeymoon before we fly back to Cairo.'

'As soon as you can arrange it,' said Leonie.

Someone tapped on the door and then Marcia put her head round it, her face mischievous. 'Is it okay if I interrupt? I ought to be starting supper soon, time's getting on, and although you two may not feel the pangs of hunger, I'm afraid I'm more earthly and I'm starving.'

'Oh, come in,' said Greg, grinning, and his sister slid into the room, eyeing them with enjoyment.

'You two are very secretive,' she said. 'Not a hint! You might have dropped a clue or two. There wasn't even any confetti in your hair, Greg.'

'Ah,' Greg said slowly. 'Talking about confetti, Marcia, you'd better buy some, you're going to need it.'

She had opened the fridge and was inspecting the contents with a jaundiced eye. 'I haven't got much in the way of wedding breakfast material, I'm afraid, how would egg and bacon do?' She looked over her shoulder vaguely. 'What was that you said, Greg? What do you mean, I'll need some confetti?'

'Leonie and I have just decided to get married,' said Greg, and his sister gave a squawk of bemused amazement.

'What? But . . .'

'It's a long story,' said Greg, sitting down on a chair. He pulled Leonie on to his lap and she curled up, her head on his shoulder, as he began to talk.

Harlequin Plus

A WORD ABOUT THE AUTHOR

Since she began writing for Harlequin Presents in late 1978, Charlotte Lamb has had close to forty books in this series published. Her explanation for this tremendous volume of superb romance writing is simple: "I love to write, and it comes very easily to me."

Once Charlotte has begun a story, the plot, the actions and the personalities of the characters unfold effortlessly and spontaneously, as her quick fingers commit the ideas of her fertile imagination to paper.

And so, in her beautiful old home on the rain-swept, uncrowded Isle of Man, where she lives with her husband and five children, Charlotte spends eight hours a day at her typewriter spinning love stories—and enjoying every minute of it!

Her career as a writer has opened many doors for her, and travel is one of them. Yet despite all the countries she has visited and enjoyed in the past few years, her greatest love is still London, the city where she was born and raised.

FREE!

A hardcover Romance Treasury volume
containing 3 treasured works of romance
by 3 outstanding Harlequin authors...

...as your introduction to Harlequin's
Romance Treasury subscription plan!

Romance Treasury

...almost 600 pages of exciting romance reading
every month at the low cost of $6.97 a volume!

A wonderful way to collect many of Harlequin's most beautiful love
stories, all originally published in the late '60s and early '70s.
Each value-packed volume, bound in a distinctive gold-embossed
leatherette case and wrapped in a colorfully illustrated dust jacket,
contains...
• 3 full-length novels by 3 world-famous authors of romance fiction
• a unique illustration for every novel
• the elegant touch of a delicate bound-in ribbon bookmark...
  and much, much more!

Romance Treasury

...for a library of romance you'll treasure forever!

Complete and mail today the FREE gift certificate and subscription
reservation on the following page.